A DISTANT VOICE

MYDWORTH MYSTERIES #9

Neil Richards • Matthew Costello

RED DOG

UK

Originally published as an eBook edition by Bastei Lübbe
AG, Cologne, Germany, 2021.

Edited by Eleanor Abraham
Cover Design by Oliver Smyth

ISBN 978-1-913331-18-4

www.reddogpress.co.uk

1.

AN INTIMATE GATHERING

NICOLA GREEN LOCKED the front door of the Women's Voluntary Service office as the bell of St Thomas tolled the hour. She turned to take in the empty Market Square on this mild June evening.

On the corner, outside the King's Arms, the usual six o'clock crowd stood – or leaned against the pub wall – sipping their pints in the still-warm sun. A low hub of chatter, the working day over, the summer evening *perfect*.

She glanced up. No rain tonight for sure. Wisps of cloud barely moved in the pale blue sky.

Across the square, she saw the usual little cluster of children, squatting in the dusty gutter of the cobbled High Street, playing marbles. Most of the shops had already shut, though she did spy Mrs Masters, rolling up the blinds of the haberdashers, pulling the shutters closed for the evening.

Over by the bank, she could see workmen already setting up the traditional trestle stage for the Mydworth Midsummer Festival, due to start on Friday.

That stage, with its garlands of foliage and brightly decorated summery wreaths, would be the bustling focus of a long weekend's entertainment – Morris dancers, mummers, musicians, mystery players, and who knew what other strange and magical surprises the people of Mydworth would manage to concoct!

Sunday would be most civilised: the Flower Show (*for which she had high hopes this year*); Tea at the Vicarage; the Children's Boat Races down on the river.

But for many, the real highlight was Saturday – Midsummer's Eve – when a great crowd would march in costume from this square, straight up to Myers Hill, fuelled by endless gallons of ale and mead, carrying the papier-mâché effigy of George's dragon *which they would burn on a great funeral pyre.*

The Summer Equinox seemed to Nicola to bring out a peculiarly ancient – even primitive – behaviour in the people of Mydworth.

And despite all the high spirits – the fun, the fire, the costumes – over the years, she'd got used to dealing with the aftermath of this chaotic event.

For some, the unsavoury effects of too much ale, too much whisky, would leave her patching up the damage.

The womenfolk of the village, too often the unwitting casualties.

But, for now – as she crossed the deserted, peaceful square – she had other things to worry about.

Amazingly enough… *matters spiritual.*

SKIRTING THE TOWN Hall, Nicola turned into Petersfield Road and followed it, past the last huddled line of workers' cottages, then crossed over onto Spa Road.

This road – actually little more than a lane – was, she knew, a dead end, leading eventually to the dense woods and fields of the old Wetherby estate.

Little trace of the original Wetherby Manor remained. Just some ghostly ruins up in the woods, and the ornate Wetherby Mausoleum below Myers Hill.

But the Grange – the more recent family home of the Wetherbys – a modest four-storey Georgian house, still stood at the end of this lane.

Nicola had never been inside the house, but tonight, she had an invitation. To a very special gathering.

One that troubled her.

The letter had come from Alice Wetherby herself, and though Nicola was used to hearing all manner of family troubles and traumas in her role running the WVS, this invitation was, for her, a definite first.

It was an invitation to a séance – *to be conducted by the* "celebrated medium Bellamy Smythe".

Nicola had heard of Bellamy Smythe. Who hadn't in this part of Sussex?

He'd been touring the county since the spring, filling town halls to bursting with his "spiritual gatherings", the crowds eager to make contact with the "other side".

Quite understandable: she knew that there were few families in England that had not been touched by the horrors of the Great War. Even now – more than a decade after Armistice Day – for some, the desire to make contact with the dead was as intense as ever.

Sometimes, she thought, *that desire seems almost like a fever. A collective madness.*

Because, no matter how many times these "mediums" were exposed as charlatans, employing time-worn tricks and smoke and mirrors to fool the gullible – there were always more desperate, grieving, sad souls prepared to pay for the slightest glimmer of hope of contact.

Nicola had known the second she had finished reading that letter, that she would go, indeed – that she *had to* go.

Her thought: *Alice Wetherby trusted her. A sympathetic shoulder to cry on.*

And now here she was, standing at the rusty, ornamental gates that led to the Grange, ready to enter and, perhaps, unmask, if necessary, a fraudster and manipulator of sad, damaged, gullible folk.

Bellamy Smythe – you'd better look out! she thought, looking up at the gaunt grey building – its peeling paint and tattered curtains in dusty windows adding to a general air of neglect.

"Seen better days this old place, hasn't it?" came a male voice behind her. "Must have been right posh, though, *once upon a time!*"

She turned to see a young man in a faded country suit and waistcoat, a cheery grin on his face, a lock of black hair drooping over his forehead. *Could this possibly be Bellamy Smythe?* she wondered. "Abel Coates, at your service," he said, making a mock military salute, then sticking out his hand. Nicola paused before taking it. *A salute? Really?*

"Nicola Green," she said. "I don't believe we've met."

"Oh, I *know* we haven't," said Abel, cheerily. "I'd certainly remember a pretty lady like you, that's for sure."

Nicola didn't react. *Smarminess.* Never attractive. And with her lack of response, Abel, for a second, looked uncertain.

"Ahem. Well, anyway. I'm the new barman, down at the Station Inn? That place, not *your* cup of tea, I imagine?"

"Oh, appearances can be deceptive, Mr Coates. I've had the occasional drink down at the Station. I run the Women's Voluntary Service. It's nearby. No airs about the place, that's for sure."

"Women's Voluntary? Ha! I can play the Trumpet Voluntary. Same tune?"

Again, Nicola didn't respond and the man suddenly looked serious.

"Sorry about that. Can't help it. Always making silly jokes, I am – especially when I'm nervous."

"Nervous?" said Nicola. Then she realised. *This man must be here for the séance too.*

"This thing?" he said, frowning and running his hand through his hair. "Tonight... all this spirit malarky... summoning the dead? I'll be honest, the very thought gives me the heebie-jeebies, it does."

Abel reinforced that thought with a visible shiver.

Nicola nodded at the man's attempt at self-disclosure. She wondered what he knew about the gathering tonight, who the others were, and why were they all invited.

But then she saw a little red Austin 7 heading towards them, speeding down the lane. As it approached, it hooted its horn loudly and turned into the drive of the Grange – *straight towards them.*

It looked as if it wasn't going to stop. Nicola and Abel jumped out of the way sharply.

As the car passed through the gates, Nicola recognised the driver – Alice's sister Christabel Taylor. Next to her, crammed into the tiny space, sat a much younger woman with bobbed hair and a bright red dress, whose eyes seemed to linger on Abel as they sped by, far too fast.

Together Nicola and Abel watched the car shoot up the drive towards the house and come to a jolting halt in a slew of gravel.

"Well, there's a sight for sore eyes," said Abel, as if Nicola – the previous target for his attention – weren't there. "I do believe my evening's beginning to look *up*."

He hurried up the drive towards the house and the car, like a hound bounding after its prey.

Nicola watched him, then followed.

Abel might be nervous about contacting the dead, but he clearly was no slouch when it came to the living.

WHEN NICOLA REACHED the front door of the Grange, the occupants of the car had already gone in – followed, no doubt, by the eager Mr Coates.

She climbed the cracked stone steps – definitely in need of repair – and went in through the half-open door into a dark, musty-smelling entrance hall.

Nobody greeted her.

No servant, no sign of Alice Wetherby. She looked around, her eyes adapting to the gloomy darkness. Underfoot, a once grand marble floor. A carpeted staircase – looking faded even in the scant light – swept upwards in a graceful curve under an enormous, cobwebbed chandelier.

Grand portraits lined the walls – but Nicola could see they, too, were all dusty and edged with cobwebs. She knew that in recent years Alice Wetherby had fallen on hard times – and now she could see the clear evidence with her own eyes.

Somewhere deep in the building, she thought she heard the sound of low conversation.

She shivered suddenly. Somehow, in spite of the warm evening, the air was chilly in here.

Then a door opened, and she saw Alice Wetherby appear.

Nicola had not seen the woman for over a year, and was surprised by how she seemed to have... *aged.*

Though probably barely in her thirties, her grey hair and Edwardian dress made her look twenty years older.

"My dear Nicola!" said Alice, hurrying across and taking Nicola's right hand in both of hers. "Has Lance not been looking after you? Greeting you? Oh, that boy, he's *worse* than useless. Tell you. I shall have to—"

"Not to worry, Alice. I've only just arrived," said Nicola, wanting to spare this Lance – whoever he was – a punishment. She realised that Alice was still holding her hand and peering intently at her. The moment turning *awkward.*

"I'm so very grateful that you've come," said Alice.

"I'm always happy to see you, Alice," said Nicola. "Though I must admit, I'm not sure about—"

"Oh, yes. I know. A séance? You *must* think me ridiculous."

"Not at all," said Nicola. "The urge to make contact with those we love is deep and genuine. Not ridiculous, but perhaps..."

"Foolhardy? Ill-advised? Gullible?"

Nicola didn't answer for a few seconds. Those were indeed the words she wanted to use. Perhaps *expensive* as well?

"You see, *that* is precisely why I invited you, Nicola," said Alice. "I know you're a sceptic. Always have been. But this time – *this time* – I know I shall finally make contact. I feel it in my very *soul.*"

Nicola stared into Alice's eyes – so bright, so impassioned.

"I don't know, Alice. All these years you've been trying, failing, getting nowhere—"

"But, Nicola, this time I have witnessed it for myself! Bellamy bridging the divide, speaking to a lost soul! It was breathtaking! Astonishing!"

"Oh! So, you've already had a séance with him?" said Nicola, concerned.

"Yes, in the private room at the Green Man. Last week. He crossed the divide, the spirits spoke!"

"To you?"

"No. To another believer. She's actually here tonight. Hoping to speak again to her dear departed husband. But Bellamy is confident that I, too, shall hear from those voices I have missed for so many years."

The woman took a deep breath, and, with that, finally released Nicola's hand.

"And when that happens, I want – no, I *need* – you here to confirm it as true."

Before Nicola could react, Alice turned and briskly crossed the marble floor to the staircase.

"For their sakes, as well as mine," continued Alice, pointing up to one of the dingy portraits on the wall. In the gloom, Nicola could make out the form of a grey-haired, moustachioed man in full dress uniform, so many medals on his chest, his bearing proud.

Seated in front of the man in the painting, on either side, two younger men, also in uniform, one holding a scroll with some Latin words.

Nicola had seen photographs of Alice's father Major Arthur Wetherby and her two brothers, James and John, before – and she recognised them now.

"It's a fine portrait," she said.

"It was painted just before they left for France. Daddy was *so* proud. He expected them all to be home in just a few months. But he never returned. Nor did my brothers. His beloved sons."

"I'm so very sorry," said Nicola – words she had used many times to Alice over the years, as the woman had poured out her grief in the little WVS office above the town square.

Not that Alice had been the only such woman. Mydworth was home to many such stories. As was probably every village in Britain. *The Great War,* they called it. *With nothing at all "great" about it.*

"All these years, I have *longed* to speak to him. And to James and John. If only to bid them farewell."

Nicola nodded, waited. The woman's desire for this impossible thing – overwhelming.

"And tonight you really believe you will?"

"I *know* it," said Alice, turning to face Nicola.

Nicola could see in her eyes, now suddenly lit and intense, that she did indeed believe this – fiercely.

And she wondered, *How can I possibly tell her that, even before it begins, this is sure to be a hoax?*

That, sadly, the dead do not speak from beyond the grave.

2.

IS THERE ANYBODY THERE?

NICOLA SAT IN the corner of the drawing room of the Grange, and looked around at the other guests in the fading sunlight from the net-curtained windows.

She had been introduced to them all by Alice, who then left them to their own devices, disappearing through double doors to help Mr Smythe prepare the dining room for tonight's "conversation with the other side".

As for Mr Smythe, he himself had not yet made an appearance.

Presumably, thought Nicola, *to heighten the drama when he finally does.*

Stagecraft, pure and simple.

This room, like the hallway, smelled stale and unused. On every wall, dark Victorian landscapes in heavy frames leaned in precariously on ancient chains.

Cobwebs hung in all the corners; the Grange's spiders clearly enjoying life here.

At one point, Nicola even saw a mouse brazenly emerge from under a bookcase and scuttle around three sides of the room before disappearing in the direction of the hallway.

On the dusty velvet-covered sofa opposite, sat Alice Wetherby's sister Christabel: thin-nosed, bird-like, silent and clearly ill at ease. Her hands were clasped in her lap; her whole bearing speaking of tension and tightness.

Next to her sat her daughter Diana – just introduced – the rather pretty red-dressed girl from the car. She was, the girl offered, just eighteen. *A little young to be talking to the dead*, Nicola thought. For her part, despite the evening's agenda, Diana looked utterly bored. Nicola saw that the young woman had taken notice of Abel Coates, though, who was standing by the bare, ash-strewn fireplace.

For a while, Coates had been the only man in the room, until the rather hangdog youth named Lance had appeared, pushing a rickety trolley of tea and biscuits.

Diana had ignored Lance, the servant *obviously* not worthy of her attention. Abel Coates, at his position by the dormant fireplace, kept gazing at the young girl. He was all smiles as he opened a silver cigarette case, lit one, and exhaled a cloud of smoke that seemed like a bit of a flirt in itself.

Diana nervously toyed with a button on her blouse and crossed her legs.

The woman next to Nicola had introduced herself as Maeve O'Connor: a hand extended for a dainty shake, a gentle smile, and with what sounded like a Dublin accent.

Not someone Nicola had actually met before. But she recognised the woman as an employee at *Salon Maurice*, Mydworth's most stylish ladies' hairdressers – not that Nicola could ever afford to have her hair done there!

When Nicola took her seat, Maeve had breathlessly informed her that her husband Liam – lost at sea in 1914 – had "crossed the divide" the other night at the Green Man and "made contact".

Nicola could see her face still flushed, eyes bright, with the excitement that Liam might return and speak to her again tonight.

She heard a clock *chime* somewhere deep in the house: a sombre eight strikes.

"I *say*," said Abel, loudly addressing the whole room. "Does anybody know when this little party is meant to kick off? So far, feels more like a wake!"

"My dear sir!" said Christabel. "I would be grateful if you would keep your opinions to yourself."

"Free world," said Abel, from his position at the fireplace. "Least, it was last time I looked."

Nicola saw him wink at Diana, who looked away. "What do you think, sweetheart?" he said. "I mean, evening like this, you should be out having fun, not sitting here in the dark."

"What my daughter should – or should *not* – be doing," said Christabel, "is absolutely no business of yours, young man."

"Hear that?" said Abel, to the room in general, taking another cigarette from his case and dramatically lighting it with a match which he then flicked into the grate. "Right proper killjoy, *now ain't she?*"

Nicola saw him wink at Diana, who blushed. And fidgety Maeve, clearly embarrassed, looked down into her lap. Christabel turned sharply, as if ready to do battle.

But before that argument could fully ignite, Nicola saw the double doors to the dining room swing wide open – and yes… *Bellamy Smythe himself entered.*

NICOLA HAD BEEN expecting someone elderly, eccentric – unsavoury even. But Smythe was anything but. He was young – in his early thirties perhaps – tall, dark haired, in a well-cut charcoal suit.

And with the most amazing, piercing blue eyes.

As he stood motionless in front of the open doors, the dark room behind him lit only by candles, Nicola was transfixed. And she realised that every other occupant of the room had been stilled too.

His sheer *presence. And that dramatic entrance…*

Nicola realised she hadn't taken a breath for some seconds. Bellamy Smythe gently moved his head, turning his gaze slowly, carefully from one guest to another, making eye contact with each and every one.

Like a priest addressing his beloved congregation.

Or a predator chancing upon a herd of innocent gazelles at a waterhole, and contemplating which one to have as an hors d'oeuvre.

"My dear *friends*," he said, his voice so soft and comforting. "How delighted I am to meet you and to know that I have such worthy companions on this evening's journey... *to the other side.*"

Nicola swallowed. *Whatever is going on here,* she thought, *it's certainly theatrical enough!*

She saw the others – even Diana – looking spellbound by this man.

No wonder people queue up to see his shows every weekend, thought Nicola. *He's like a movie star!*

"I do hope those of you who are expecting to make contact with lost ones tonight have brought – as asked – a memento to focus the spirit plane?" said Bellamy now, his eyes again glancing across the room.

Nicola saw some nods, as Maeve opened her handbag, and Abel began rummaging in his pockets. Bellamy raised his hand, and the room froze again.

"Well then, my new friends, it is *time*. Let us begin."

With that, Nicola saw him turn on his heels and melt back through the double doors into the darkened room. In his place, Alice appeared from the shadows and nervously beckoned them all to join her.

"Quickly now," she said in a hushed voice. "Bellamy told me there is *already* electrical activity! He says the spirits may be gathering – and they are eager to cross the divide!"

Nicola stood, and waited as the others hurried into the dark room. Then, with a nod to Alice, she followed.

As she crossed the threshold into the dining room, she saw Lance step past her, and heard the double doors behind her slide tightly shut.

NICOLA SHIVERED AS a waft of cool, damp air brushed the back of her neck.

For twenty minutes now, she had sat at the velvet-draped dining table, her hands on the table, as instructed, the little fingers on each touching the little fingers of the other guests at her side – Alice to her left, her sister Christabel to her right.

On Christabel's other side, sat her daughter Diana. Before the candles were dimmed, Nicola had seen the young woman sighing and yawning – still clearly wishing to be anywhere but here in this fusty old house.

Abel sat at Diana's right. Nicola had had to restrain herself from laughing out loud at his hurried manoeuvrings, eager to ensure he sat next to the young woman.

Maeve sat directly across from Diana. Finally, to complete the circle on Abel's other side, Bellamy sat – with one hand touching the barman's and the other touching Maeve's.

When they had all finally taken their seats, the servant Lance had extinguished the candles one by one until only the lone candle in the centre of the round table remained lit, its flickering light positioned perfectly to light one face and one face only.

Bellamy Smythe.

After a minute's silence, he had called upon the spirits to make themselves known. But so far, although he had tried to make contact with the various relatives of the guests, nobody had come forward.

A bit of reluctance, it would seem, in the spirit world!

Bellamy had then gone around the table, asking each guest to name the spirit they wished to contact.

Abel, abandoning his rakish pose, said quietly that he desired a word from his dear spouse, Betty, departed in 1919, taken by the Spanish flu.

But, so far, not a word from good old Betty.

Maeve was desperate to hear again from her beloved husband, Liam.

But Liam, it would seem, had other matters to attend to tonight.

Nicola – playing along but expecting no RSVP – named her own long-departed mother, Margaret. But her mum also declined to make an appearance, in spite of the fact Nicola had asked as sweetly as she knew how.

So far, she thought, *Bellamy's séance is a flop.*

Nicola guessed she was the only one not surprised. She herself hadn't expected to meet any spirits tonight at all – let alone her dear old mum, who in life had been sceptical of nearly everything and everyone.

She looked across the candle's flare at Bellamy, whose gaze now locked on her.

Maybe he'll have more luck with Alice, she thought. *After all, she's paying for this little charade.*

But Bellamy's compelling eyes did not move on.

"You think this is a *charade*, Nicola?" said Bellamy, smiling at her. "I can assure you, it *isn't.*"

Nicola took a sharp breath. *What? How in heaven's name did he know what she had been thinking?*

"Indeed," he continued. "I do believe that the spirits of the departed Wetherbys will make themselves known… *now.*"

Nicola shivered as another draught of icy air swept across her neck, and she felt Christabel move at her side.

"Oh! I just felt something cold!" she said. "Right behind me!"

"Alice," said Bellamy, his voice deep, serious. "Please tell us who you wish to contact."

"My father," said Alice, at Nicola's side. "The Major."

Bellamy's voice now rose in volume. "We call now upon any spirits who are here in this house who wish to converse with Alice Wetherby! Please – give us a sign that you are among us!"

Nothing. Silence in the room, apart from the steady breathing of the group. Nicola could hear a wind kicking up outside. And then the sound of rain hitting the windows behind the heavy curtains.

Funny, she thought. *That afternoon sky had been so clear! No hint of a storm coming.*

"Is there *anybody* there?" called Bellamy again, even louder.

This time – as clear and close as if it came from just inches in front of her – Nicola heard a loud *tap, tap, tap* upon the table.

At the same time, the candle on the table flared brighter, and everyone jolted back in their seats – Nicola included.

"Please, dear friends, you must relax," said Bellamy, and Nicola could see him smiling in the candlelight. "Remain calm, and breathe deeply. It is so very important!"

Around the table, Nicola saw the other participants nod and try to obey.

All the hands still visible, still joined. *How had Bellamy made that noise?*

"Yes. Quite natural to feel fear," said Bellamy. "But remember, the spirits… they, *too,* are nervous."

The candle dimmed again, and Bellamy's eyes, catching that flickering light, raised to the ceiling.

"Do we have a spirit with us?" he said. "Tap again if you are there."

A pause, and then a single tap sounded – and now, to Nicola, it seemed to come from behind her. She felt goosebumps on her arms.

Ridiculous, she thought. *Just trickery.*

And yet…

"Spirit – do you wish to speak to Alice Wetherby?"

Tap.

"Identify yourself, spirit, please! Are you Major Wetherby? One tap for yes, two for no."

Another *tap* – this time, it seemed, from the very centre of the table.

Nicola heard Alice cry out, and saw her raise her hand to her mouth.

"Please," said Bellamy. "I must warn you. Do *not* break the circle."

Nicola felt Alice's fingers touch hers again.

"Father!" said Alice. "I—I'm here!"

"Well, we can all hear that," came Abel's voice from across the table.

"Everyone – save the person contacted – quiet, please, *everybody,*" said Bellamy.

A DISTANT VOICE

A flash of lightning illuminated the whole room, then a few seconds later came a crash of thunder. *Did Bellamy order up a convenient storm as well? What was going on?* "Blimey," said Abel, his bravado apparently diminished. "You know what? I don't like this, don't like this at all."

"Shhh!" said Maeve. "You *heard* Mr Smythe! You'll break the spell!"

Bellamy had now closed his eyes. Then, slowly, as if taking care with each word, he said, "Do you have a message for your daughters, Major?"

Nicola felt the room turn cold. Was it her imagination, or...? *Was that actually fog drifting low across the room?*

Another tap – this one as loud as if a ruler had been slapped down upon a desk – and Nicola thought she felt the table shake.

And now, yet another flash of lightning, the thunder almost immediate! The candle flame flickered then roared upwards again, shooting sparks onto the tablecloth.

The thunder came rolling on, rumbling, as if – Nicola thought – *as if it wasn't natural.*

"I'm scared, Mr Smythe," said Diana, her voice surprisingly loud over the infernal noise that now seemed to be filling the whole house.

"You have nothing to fear!" said Bellamy. "Remember, if we do as they say, if we keep the circle unbroken, the spirits will not harm us!"

"But... but what does the damn thing *want?*" cried Abel.

"Yes, what do you want?" Alice dared to say. "Tell me, father! What do you want? *Speak to me!*"

"Spirit, we ask – nay, we implore you – give us your message!" called out Bellamy.

And then everything seemed to Nicola to happen at once.

Bellamy's head rocked back so far that his chin pointed almost at the ceiling, and Nicola saw his blue eyes roll upwards into his head leaving just the whites visible – the image so gruesome, so unnatural.

And – as if controlled like some kind of puppet – his mouth so very slowly drew open, lips bared against white teeth, and a gurgling, guttural sound emerged from the back of this throat.

No, not a *sound*. *A voice*.

But not a natural voice, not Bellamy's voice – but instead, some supernatural form of distorted, echoing, hissing voice, yes, still recognisable to Nicola as a man's voice, but at the same time seemingly *not a living man's voice*.

"Alice," said the voice, as if struggling to form the words. "Oh, my dear child."

"Daddy?" said Alice, and Nicola saw her eyes widen in the candlelight. "Is that really-"

"And Christabel. Oh! You're here too!" came the voice. "Oh... both my girls, my bonny girls..."

Alice stood – *breaking the circle*.

"Daddy!" she shrieked. "Daddy!"

A great gust of wind rocked the house, and the heavy, drawn curtains blew away from the French windows.

Lightning flashed again, filling the room with light so bright that Nicola was, for a few seconds, blinded. With a loud CRACK the doors themselves were *flung* open, glass panes shattering, scattering the whole group, who rose from the table and backed away, some screaming.

And then in an instant, the wind magically just *ceased,* and Nicola saw Lance at the open door, his face looking shocked, his hand on the electric light switch, the room illuminated again.

The wind quieted. The thunder turned distant. The giant bolts of lightning fading away as well.

Bellamy suddenly slumped forward, his head almost banging the table.

As the participants stood in shock, still reeling, Nicola saw Alice standing alone, swaying, her face pale, her eyes wide, horrified, as her hands began to claw at the air as if grasping for support.

And then *she* pitched forward and crashed into the table, slumped to the ground in a dead faint.

A DISTANT VOICE

As if awakening from a dream, Nicola rushed to Alice, reaching out, her heart pounding, trying to understand what had just happened.

She had arrived a sceptic. But now, with all of this?

Overwhelming.

3.

A MOST STRANGE CASE BEGINS

SIR HARRY MORTIMER strolled down Mydworth High Street in the early morning sunshine, doffing his hat and nodding "good mornings" to the shopkeepers as they opened up for this very special Friday, pulling down canvas awnings, setting out window displays.

He always *loved* this time of day: the cobbles spick and span (not so many horses yet!), the air so clear, the stifling June heat still hours away.

And this week in particular – the week of the Midsummer Festival – there was always that mysterious spirit underlying everything.

All the way down the street, into the square at the foot of the hill, he spotted garlands of flowers looped along the shop fronts, and colourful summery wreaths decorating every doorway. At Sunday's Flower Show, he knew, there would be judging and prize-giving and he would probably be asked (yet again) to take part.

How could one say no?

Into the square now, already busy with the early travelling stalls – fishmonger, butcher, baker – all bringing the best of Sussex to the village. And he noticed the newly erected stage at the far end for the evening shows.

A concert every night for three nights: folk music, mummers, Morris dancers and – though there was a spirited debate about this non-traditional choice, he had heard – a real jazz band for Sunday.

This weekend will be quite the eye-opener for Kat, he thought. No doubt his wife would never have seen anything quite like Mydworth's summer festival back in her native New York.

He stopped and looked up at the first-floor bay window of the Women's Voluntary Service, where Kat worked a couple of days a week, helping local women and families when times were hard and – sometimes – their marriages harder.

Mostly the latter, he knew.

Sure enough, there she was, standing at the window, coffee cup cradled in her hands. She gave him a smile and a wave and he headed down the narrow alley between the terraced shops, that led to the stairs up to the WVS office.

He wondered just what had prompted her urgent telephone call to him back at the house, barely five minutes into her morning's shift.

Something, apparently, was up.

Well, he thought, *I imagine I'm about to find out.*

KAT HAD THE door open as Harry reached the top of the stairs, and she gave him a kiss as she let him into the office.

"Sorry, didn't we just do that half an hour ago?" he said, smiling and removing his hat. "Not that I'm complaining, of course."

"A good marriage can *never* have enough kissing," said Nicola Green, rising from her desk in the corner and coming over to shake Harry's hand.

"Now, you see, *that* kind of advice is exactly why I support this charity," said Harry, putting his hat on the stand. He smiled at his wife. "And, of course, the fact that Kat works here."

"Harry, take a seat. This may take a while," said Nicola, then she turned and called through to the back office where her young assistant worked. "Melissa, my dear, when you have a moment? Teas and coffees please."

Kat joined Harry at the table while they waited for Melissa.

"Have you seen the square? said Nicola. "Midsummer here again! There'll be some wassailing tonight, for sure."

"Wassailing?" said Kat, raising her eyes at Harry.

"I'll explain later," said Harry, laughing. "Not to worry, it's a very *safe* activity. Usually."

"And I imagine," continued Nicola, "this being just the beginning of the festival weekend, it'll be fairly tame."

"Harry's been educating me about mummers, Morris dancers and even papier-mâché beasts," said Kat. "I *still* can't decide if he's 'having me on' or not."

"Whatever he's told you, rest assured, it'll be stranger than you can possibly imagine," said Nicola. "And probably twice as fun."

"Teas and coffees, and biscuits," said Melissa, putting the tray on the table, then turning to go. "I'll leave you to pour, Nicola."

"Let me guess," said Harry, when Melissa had left the room. "Is it to do with the mysterious séance that took place on Wednesday?"

"*You* must be psychic," said Nicola, pouring the tea.

"These days, who isn't?" said Kat, taking a cup and smiling. "Truth is our housekeeper Maggie, gave us the lowdown over breakfast – or, at least, the story according to the Mydworth gossip machine."

"*That* machine... never the most reliable of sources," said Harry. "But the nub of it, as I understand it, is that there were mysterious, even scary, goings on in the middle of one of those dreadful séances. That about right?"

"That part is true enough," said Nicola. "And I should know – because I was there myself."

"Ah," said Harry. "I'm sorry – when I said 'dreadful' I didn't mean to imply, er—"

"Oh, don't you worry about *that*, Harry," said Nicola. "You see, I was there on the bidding of one of my clients: Alice Wetherby."

"So, you saw the whole shebang?" said Harry. "I gather the evening had a rather dramatic finale."

"Terrifying is the word I would use," said Nicola. "And, well, to me at least, inexplicable."

"Really?" said Harry, sipping his tea. "The way I heard it, your Alice Wetherby had an unexpected tête-à-tête with her deceased father?"

"Well, that's one way of describing it, Sir Harry, for sure," said Nicola.

"*You* clearly believe there's something up, or we wouldn't be having this meeting, am I right?" he said.

"Yes, I do. Somehow..." said Nicola, "I think there's something extremely shady going on, with dear Alice Wetherby potentially being the victim."

"Well, that doesn't sound good," said Harry.

"Nicola," said Kat, "why don't you tell Harry what you just told me about what happened that night – from the beginning?"

With a nod, Nicola began.

KAT WATCHED HARRY as he listened carefully, and took notes, while Nicola Green related the events of Wednesday evening at the Grange. When she'd finished, he sat back and reflected for a minute.

Kat knew he was thinking through the permutations of the strange happenings that night.

"Okay. Alice has a bit of a track record for this kind of thing, yes?" he said, finally, breaking the silence.

"Over the years, she's pretty much tried everything – and *everyone*. Séances. Hypnosis. All to contact her deceased father. None of them worked, of course."

"Cost her a pretty penny, though, I bet."

"Indeed."

"So, what's different this time?"

Kat saw Nicola think for a few seconds before answering.

"Not exactly sure, Harry. But it feels as if this chap Bellamy's in some way... *targeting* her."

"Go on," said Harry.

"It started a few weeks ago, apparently. He invited her to come to a séance at his hotel. Out of the blue, apparently."

"Interesting," said Harry. "So that led to this séance in her own home?"

"Yes."

"All right," said Harry. "Let's go back to Wednesday night. You say you actually heard the old Major speaking out?" he said.

"Well, through Bellamy. I believe they call it 'channelling'. The voice distorted, strange." She took a breath. "Sounds ridiculous, doesn't it? But it certainly persuaded Alice. She was completely convinced it was her father talking to her."

Harry nodded, made a note.

"And what about the flashing lights, the bangs, doors blowing open, glass breaking and such? Couldn't that just have been the storm? Certainly was quite a zinger, you know – nearly took the roof off our summerhouse!"

"The storm was real enough," said Nicola. "But what happened was more than a storm."

"Aha! You don't think it was the work of ghosts and ghouls?" said Harry, smiling. "Those nasty things that go bump in the night?"

"I didn't say that," said Nicola, smiling.

"Right. Trickery then? *Deception?*"

"There's no other explanation," said Nicola, "is there?"

"No," said Harry, shaking his head firmly, "not in my universe. Say, Kat, you have such things in the Bronx?"

And his wife laughed. "The Bronx has far more serious things to be concerned about. But let's say we *are* talking *deception* – then the first question is *how*, and then *why.*"

"I was rather hoping you two would be able to tell me that," said Nicola, laughing.

"Oh, we will," said Harry. "I don't doubt it. Or maybe that sounds a tad too confident. But we'll do our level best."

Kat turned to Nicola. "You say Alice's servant switched on the electric light when the séance stopped? Did you notice if everyone was still in the same place where they had originally been seated at the table?"

"More or less. They were now standing, of course."

"But nobody had moved?"

"No."

"Then whatever made the French windows blow in, it couldn't have been Bellamy or the other participants?"

He waited while Nicola thought about this.

"No. I don't think so. I mean, nobody was even close."

"What if Bellamy had wires?" said Harry. "Some kind of cables set up?"

"I think I would have seen," said Nicola. "In fact, I'm sure I would. I was on the lookout for exactly that kind of thing."

"Okay then, what about the strange tapping?" said Kat. "Could Bellamy have set something up under the table to do that?"

"Possible," said Nicola. "Though the sound seemed to echo from all over the room."

Kat watched Harry nod at that and make another note in his book.

"Now, tell me about the voice," he said. "The deceased Major Wetherby."

"The voice. Oh, that really did *sound* as if it came from beyond the grave."

"I'm sure. These crafty people are masters of the dark arts. The dark arts of theatre, usually."

"Well, there was no shortage of theatre at the Grange that night, I can tell you," said Nicola.

"Certainly sounds that way," said Harry. "I think Kat and I will need a plan of the table from you – who sat where, and so on?"

"Of course," said Nicola, taking a sheet of paper from a stack on the table, and a pen. "I can do that now."

"Also, a list of the participants, their names and whatever you know about them."

Nicola nodded again. "You two do agree... this is rather odd? Even... ominous?" she said, writing.

"I certainly do, on both counts," said Harry. "But what I just can't fathom is *motive*. This kind of thing... staged, scary, and clearly focussed on one person. There's usually some kind of grifting at the bottom of it. But you said Alice and Christabel are totally on their uppers, that right?"

"Uppers?" Kat said.

"Ah," said Harry, smiling. "Means no money, or certainly very little."

"The family *used* to have money, back in the day," said Nicola. "But after Alice lost her father, I heard there were heavy death duties. They had to sell most of their land. Get rid of the staff."

"Yes. So, whatever he's after, it's got to be more than just the fee for the séance?" said Harry.

"That can't be more than five or ten guineas anyway," said Nicola.

Kat looked at Harry, who could clearly guess what she was thinking, and nodded.

Who would set up a big scam — lights, windows, theatrical effects — for just a few guineas?

"Kat – your thoughts?" said Harry. "At first glance, it certainly seems there's some slippery and dubious work afoot."

Kat nodded. "Yes. But what that is – and why – we haven't a clue about yet."

"*Clues* indeed! Always useful in matters such as this."

Kat turned back to Nicola.

"We'll need to talk to people," said Kat. "Alice Wetherby, her sister, the niece Diana, right? This guy Bellamy Smythe... and so on."

"Yes. And how have the two sisters reacted?" said Harry.

"Christabel Taylor, the younger sister, seems to have locked herself away at home and not come out," said Nicola. "She's a bit of a recluse apparently, anyway."

"Husband not around?" said Harry. "I mean – name of Taylor?"

"Lost at the end of the war," said Nicola. "Like so many. Lives alone with her daughter."

"I imagine 'hearing' her father shook her up," said Kat.

"We're going to have to get around that somehow," said Harry. "What about Alice?"

"I went to see her yesterday. She's still recovering. But I have to say, she is also overjoyed at having made contact with her father."

"So, she believes that what happened was the *real* thing?" said Kat.

"*Completely*," said Nicola, shrugging. "She actually said how *thrilling* the whole evening was. In spite of the fact that she fainted clean away."

Kat looked at Harry, who raised his eyebrows.

"What about Bellamy Smythe?" he said. "What does *he* say about all this?"

"According to Alice, he is delighted with the evening's events," said Nicola.

"I bet he is," said Kat.

"I gather he's already planning another séance at the Grange," said Nicola. "Seems confident the Major will pay another visit."

"Is he now?" said Harry. "How *very* perceptive of him. Well, we shall definitely try to join Alice for that little performance."

"We should talk to him straight away, don't you think, Harry?"

"You'll be lucky," said Nicola. "He's tucked away in his rooms at the Green Man, apparently – until tonight."

"What happens tonight?" said Kat.

"Oh, his first public Mydworth show in the Town Hall, seven-thirty sharp."

"Let me guess – on the back of Wednesday's little drama, the evening's a sell-out?" said Harry.

"Tickets already going for twice the face value," said Nicola.

"Any chance you can get us a couple?" said Harry.

"Shouldn't be a problem," said Nicola. "I do have my... contacts."

Kat looked at Harry.

"So, Harry, where do we start?"

"Oh, I think a visit to the Grange, don't you?" said Harry, pushing back his chair and standing.

"I shall telephone Alice this second," said Nicola. "Tell her you're on your way."

"Great," said Kat, standing too.

"Don't forget the list of names," said Nicola, handing over a sheet of paper. "I'll find some contact details for them if I can, if you drop by the office later."

Kat turned and plucked Harry's hat from the stand, handed it to him, and together they headed down the stairs and into the square.

To the scene of the séance... and the crime.

If crime it was.

4.

A RETURN TO THE GRANGE

AS THEY MADE their way across Market Square, Kat noticed a small but noisy crowd gathered by the festival stage.

In the centre, a group of a dozen or so men in white shirts and knee hose, all of them wearing black top hats with fluffy green feathers sticking out, and carrying long sticks. She could see that some of them had pints of beer in their hands, although it was still barely mid-morning. One or two were banging out a simple rhythm on side drums as a concertina played.

"Aha, like the first cuckoo of spring," said Harry, following her gaze. "The Morris men have arrived!"

"Let me guess," said Kat. "They dance around and then hit each other with those sticks?"

"Well done! Got it in one," said Harry. "All part of our rich local history, supposedly. Though, truth is, I think it's mostly a good excuse to get away from the wife and have a few early pints of ale."

"Well, don't you go getting ideas."

"Oh, I don't *know*," said Harry, laughing. "Those outfits *are* rather fetching. Though I think I'd draw the line at wearing bells on my ankles. Think that would make me feel more like a house cat!"

"Hold onto that bell idea. I may have uses for that," said Kat, laughing too, as they left the square behind and turned into Spa Road.

"You know, this séance nonsense," said Harry. "You had it in New York too?"

"Imagine so."

"Ever go to one?"

"Sadly, no," said Kat. "But when I was a kid my dad took me to see a hypnotist at Pfaff's Theatre."

"Interesting. Let me guess – the gent had people running around thinking they were chickens? Eating soup like it was ice cream?"

"That kind of thing, sure. But there was one other act – Magic Margaret, the Mesmerist. And *that* did scare me. She seemed to know secrets about people in the audience. I was always worried she'd know my secrets too."

"Really? Innocent young thing like you – what *possible* secrets could they be?" said Harry, smiling.

"Oh, Harry, you'd be surprised. Sounds like you've seen the same kind of thing though, yes?"

"Pretty much," said Harry. "Aunt Lavinia took me to a few shows in the West End. Actually inspired me to learn some magic tricks. She used to wheel me out at Christmas to do a quick turn for all the grown-ups before dinner."

"Magic, eh? Could be useful here," said Kat.

"*Could* be. Though I suspect Bellamy Smythe is a tad more proficient – and deceptive – than I ever was!"

"You think we'll be able to find out how he did what he did at the séance?"

"Perhaps. If they didn't get rid of the evidence. Somehow, we'll need to grab a minute alone, inside that room, to investigate."

"Well, here we are, I believe," said Kat, as she saw a pair of rusty iron gates and an old metal sign hanging at an angle: "The Grange".

They passed through the gates and walked up the gravel drive, until the Grange came into view. Kat took in its tired exterior and realised that Nicola hadn't been exaggerating the run-down state of the place.

"Wow. Needs more than a lick of paint," she said.

"Certainly *does*," said Harry, and then he stopped – staring at the house.

"You look like you've seen a ghost," said Kat, "and we've not even gone in yet."

"Funny. In a way, I have," he said, turning, his blue eyes catching the light. "You see, I do believe I *know* this place."

"Always think there's hardly a place in Mydworth you *don't* know."

"Ah, see, but this is different. It's coming back to me now. I used to come here, when I was little. Whole bunch of us. To play with the Wetherby boys. John and James."

"Alice's lost brothers?"

"Indeed. Doubt she'll remember me. I must have been… eight, nine? She'd be even younger. We used to roam the gardens, bit of rule-less rugby, that sort of thing."

They carried on walking towards the house.

"A shame they didn't make it back to Blighty," said Harry. "Shame for so many young men."

Kat nodded at that, remembering – that with his plane crash – Harry had almost been one of those who didn't return home.

"You've been inside, too?"

"Oh *yes*. Old place like this? So much fun to explore, like Lavinia's house. Nothing like an attic or musty basement to hide in on a rainy day when you're a young lad."

They reached the cracked stone steps that led up to the once grand front door – the paint now peeling and faded.

"Guess it was in better shape then?" said Kat, as she reached up and pulled a handle marked "bell".

"Ha, that's for sure," said Harry as the bell echoed from deep within the house. "Those days – they certainly weren't short of money."

"Wonder what happened to it?" said Kat.

But before Harry could answer, she heard the door creak open and saw a young man peer out at them, his fingers tightly wrapped around the edge of the door.

"How many times do I have to tell you *people*?" said the man. "There's no one home to visitors!"

"Sir Harry and Lady Mortimer, to see Miss Wetherby," said Harry, politely, as if he hadn't heard the outburst.

The young man looked confused.

"You got an appointment? Nobody told me—"

"Think Miss Wetherby is expecting us," said Kat, smiling.

That seemed to do the trick – and the man opened the door wide to let them in.

KAT HADN'T BEEN expecting the interior to be so dark – but it seemed most of the curtains and shutters were closed tight.

The air smelled dusty and stale as they stood in the wide hallway. The young man shut the front door, then looked confused as to the next steps, brushing a stray lock of hair from his eyes and frowning.

In a tired suit and a white shirt with frayed collar, he seemed an unlikely servant.

"What is it, Lance?" came a loud voice from upstairs, and Kat looked up to see a young woman coming down the graceful, curving staircase, a silver tray in her hands.

"These people. They *say* they're here to see Miss Wetherby. But she didn't say anything to me about—"

Kat watched as the young woman abruptly handed the tray to Lance.

"Take this to the kitchen," she said. Then as he did as he was told and took the tray away, she turned to them. "Sorry about that. Lance is still learning the ropes. I'm Diana."

She stuck out her hand, and Kat and Harry shook it.

"Miss Wetherby's niece?" said Harry.

"That's right."

"Do you live here?" said Kat. "I didn't realise—"

"Gosh, no! I mean, amazing place, isn't it, but what a shambles! Got mice everywhere. My God. Scary. No, I live with my mother. But I come over whenever I can, give my aunt a hand, make some soup, whatever needs doing."

"No other staff, apart from Lance?" said Harry.

"Poor old Aunt Alice, can't afford it. Lance has been here a few months. Does what he can, at a price my aunt can barely afford. But, ahem, well." She lowered her voice. "As you can see, he's not exactly the sharpest knife in the drawer."

"And you think Miss Wetherby is up to seeing us?" said Kat. "We could come back later?"

"Oh no, absolutely, it's a good time. She's looking forward to meeting you both. But probably best if it's just a *quick* chat? She's still rather fragile from the other night."

"I'm sure she is," said Kat. "You saw it all happen, I gather?"

"Saw what?" said the girl, looking confused.

"The séance," said Harry, smiling.

"Oh gosh, *that*! Didn't I just. Strangest thing I ever saw, too. Though, I've no idea what I actually *did* see, mind! All this supernatural stuff goes right over my head! Pretty spooky, though, I can tell you."

Kat smiled.

Although Diana looked every bit of her eighteen years, she still had plenty of childlike ways about her.

"I gather that's what you've come to talk to my aunt about?" she said.

"It is," said Harry.

"Well, if you're thinking of contacting the spirit world, she's certainly the expert! All she ever talks about!"

Just then, Kat saw Lance emerge from a corridor behind her, wiping his hands on a cloth.

"Ah, Lance," said Diana, "why don't you take our guests through to the drawing room and look after them. And I'll bring my aunt down."

Kat saw Lance frown at the girl.

Probably doesn't like taking orders from an eighteen-year-old, she thought.

He ushered them towards a door from the hall.

32

"Drawing room's right through here," he said, and Kat followed Harry through the door and into a large room filled with shabby worn sofas, low tables and equally sad armchairs.

Once upon a time, this had clearly been a grand reception room, but now it was tired, dark and *so* fusty.

"Er, sorry about earlier," said Lance, and Kat turned to him and smiled.

"Don't worry," she said.

"Since the other night, all *sorts* of people have been coming round wanting to know what happened. Piccadilly Circus it's been."

"Really? Who's been around?"

At that, Lance shrugged. "Dunno. People. All so curious."

"I'm sure," said Harry. "Mydworth folks – love a good ghost story, especially at Midsummer!"

Kat saw Lance grin – *poor kid's been under pressure,* she thought. Maybe just needs a bit of sympathy.

"Can't have been easy for you," she said. "The mess after the séance. Lot of nosey people. And no other staff to help out?"

"Just me," said Lance. "Miss Wetherby, she, well, you know…"

"Chief cook and bottle-washer, eh?" said Harry.

"Mostly bottle-washer," said Lance, grinning again.

"Must have been really busy on Wednesday night then?" said Kat innocently. "Tea, biscuits, drinks to serve – as well as helping Miss Wetherby to organise everything?"

"Well, she wouldn't let me near the organising. But yes, I had to do the teas. Buy the biscuits. Non-stop, it was."

"And did you see the, er, dramatic events?" said Harry.

"Nah. Just the end, when it all went a bit mad. I ran in – turned the lights on. Heard the racket. Was worried somebody had got hurt."

"You must have been frightened then?" said Kat.

"I was. A bit. Especially afterwards. When I found out they all thought that they'd been talking to bloody ghosts." Lance caught himself. "Er, sorry Lady Mort–"

"No worries."

"But you didn't hear these 'ghosts' yourself?" said Harry.

"Nah. I was doing the washing up," said Lance, his voice sounding dismal. "All them teacups, you know."

Kat smiled. He seemed to remember something. "Oh. I was supposed to ask you, if you wanted tea."

"Now, that would be lovely," said Harry, and Kat turned to him, knowing he was not usually one for cups of tea when out and about. "Tea, darling?"

"Dying for a cup," she said, getting the message.

"Make yourselves comfortable," said Lance, nodding to the uninviting armchairs and a faded leather sofa. "I'll go make some."

Kat watched him go out of the door to the hallway, then the minute he'd disappeared, she saw Harry heading for another door opposite.

"From what *I* remember, the dining room is through here," he said and winked. "The scene of the crime! Or whatever. Shall we?"

And, without waiting, he opened the door, reached in to turn on the electric light, and went through.

5.

THE SCENE OF THE CRIME?

HARRY STEPPED INTO the dining room and quickly took in the room: big, round dining table; a dozen chairs; dusty old portraits. The curtains were all tightly drawn and the place had a strong smell of candlewax, and burning.

There was a tang of something else in the air that he recognised. *Was that fireworks?*

He could see shattered glass on the floor, now in small piles as though someone had made a first attempt at cleaning it up — and then got distracted.

He had already sized up Alice Wetherby's lone helper, Lance, as someone not making *too* much of an effort to do much of anything. Then again, singlehanded in a large house like this, Harry could hardly blame the lad if he hadn't yet had time to clear up.

In terms of what Harry needed now — well — that was no bad thing.

"What are we looking for exactly?" said Kat.

He turned to see her standing in the doorway, gently closing the door behind her.

"Signs of things being tampered with," said Harry. "Anything out of the ordinary, I imagine."

"Trickery and deception?"

"*Exactly*. Shall we check the table?"

Kat lifted up the heavy table cover and they both crouched down to peer under.

"Nothing this side," said Kat.

Harry peered at the underside of the table, looking for any signs of tampering.

"Nothing here, either," he said, running his hands across the heavy wood.

Then he stopped.

"Wait a minute."

He rolled over on his back and looked up: there, tucked into a crevice in the table's frame, was a small brass eyelet. He reached up and unscrewed it, then rolled back out.

As they both stood up, he opened his palm to show Kat.

"See here? Brand new. Shiny. And there for one reason and one reason only."

"Let me guess," said Kat. "To run a fishing line through?"

"Interesting. I imagine if we had a good light we'd find the marks where more of these little fellows were hooked up."

"Well that explains how he does the table tapping," said Kat. She looked around. "What about these doors that smashed?"

Harry crossed the room and pulled back the big curtains to reveal a pair of French windows, their shattered panes covered in temporary wooden boards.

On the carpet in front of them – still more glass.

He saw a key in the lock and turned it, then gently pulled open the doors to inspect them – and as he did, Kat, with a look to the dining room door, joined him.

How many minutes would they have here?

"You think the storm blew them open – as opposed to the dreaded Dark Forces from beyond?"

He felt the heavy glass door, moved it back and forth.

"Oh – as you know – those Dark Forces, they're unstoppable. On the other hand – if these doors were *already* unlocked, it wouldn't take much. A good gust would do the trick. But hang on. What do we have here?"

He knelt down to inspect the outer stone sill. The stone was smudged with black, and he could see more black patches on the grass next to it.

He took out his handkerchief, wiped the stone, then raised it to his nose and sniffed.

"Well, that answers another question," he said, getting up and turning to Kat.

"Some kind of pyrotechnics?"

He extended the cloth to Kat.

"So it would seem, yes. At a rough guess, enough to make one hell of a blinding flash – and a bang too."

"Throw in a well-aimed kick to the base of the door from a helpful brute hiding in the bushes and you have the perfect ghostly intrusion."

"Especially with all that thunder and lightning going on too."

He stepped back into the room, shut the doors, and with Kat's help pulled the curtains closed – just as the door to the dining room opened.

Harry turned to see what he guessed was Alice Wetherby, with Diana at her side.

"Well, well," said Alice. "Sir Harry. Here again."

"Miss Wetherby," said Harry, hardly believing that this frail, grey-haired woman was the child that had played with him all those years ago. "You remember!"

She came close and took his hand, peering into his eyes.

"My brothers had great fun with you. I always wished I could have joined in." She looked away for a moment. "What a long, long time ago that was," she said. "Hard to believe so many years have flown."

"Indeed," said Harry. Then he turned. "My wife, Lady Mortimer."

"Kat," his wife added, with a quick smile.

Alice took her hand, smiled, then stepped back.

"This room... these days... hardly appropriate for entertaining," she said, turning to her niece.

"Aunt Alice, I'm sorry, I told Lance to serve them tea in the drawing room, *not* here." said Diana.

"Oh, my fault," said Harry. "We wanted to see in here. I should have waited and asked."

A DISTANT VOICE

Alice didn't miss the beat.

"Let me guess. The temptation to debunk my dear friend Bellamy, too great for you?" said Alice.

"Not at all."

Clever lady, Harry thought. *Maybe not so easily duped?*

"Oh, don't you worry," said Alice. "I *know* why dear Nicola asked you here. She doubts the evidence of her own eyes the other night. She simply has not the courage to believe."

"But *you* do?" said Kat.

"With my heart and soul."

Harry looked at Kat and nodded – an invitation for her to carry on.

"So, you don't mind then if we ask you some questions?" said Kat.

"*Not at all.*" She turned to Diana. "Please, my dear, be so kind as to ask Lance to serve tea in here."

When Diana had gone, Alice sat at the table.

"Now then, where would you like to begin?" she said, calmly.

KAT WATCHED HARRY pull out a dining chair to sit, but she decided to remain standing.

"Miss Wetherby—"

"Alice, please."

Kat smiled. "Alice, it is. So, you *know* why Nicola suggested we come to see you?"

"*Of course,*" said Alice. "She wants you to prove that Bellamy Smythe is a fraud, and – absurdly – to save me from being duped."

Kat had to admire the woman. *She certainly didn't pull her punches.*

"And you don't believe that is happening?"

"Over the years, I have seen my fair share of frauds and conmen, Kat. And Bellamy Smythe is neither."

"You mind me asking exactly *why* you believe in him?" said Kat. "I mean – was it the tapping? The doors blowing open?"

"Dear me, no, it was neither of *those* things. Although I do believe they were genuine manifestations from the spirit world."

Kat thought about this. *It only left one thing.*

"It was the voice," she said.

"Yes," said Alice, after a long pause.

"It sounded like your father."

"It did. I mean, coming through Bellamy of course. But that's not all."

Kat looked at Harry. *Where was this going?*

"You see, it wasn't *how* he spoke," said Alice. "It was what he *said.*"

"Go on," said Harry, this moment now so... *delicate.*

"When Christabel and I were little, my father used to sing us a song, in the nursery. A song he made up. Nobody else apart from my mother and the boys ever heard it. He had such a *fine* singing voice."

Kat waited as Alice stared into the distance, then heard her sing the words, so softly:

"My bonny girls, my two bonny girls..."

And Kat now realised.

"He used those very words at the séance, didn't he?" she said.

"Yes," said Alice, smiling again. "And at that moment, well, I knew it really was him."

HARRY LOOKED AT Kat. She was being so careful and gentle with this poor, broken woman.

He wasn't surprised at her next question, as Kat pulled out a chair, inspected it – probably to make sure no shards of glass lay on the seat – and then sat down.

"How did you first meet Mr Smythe?" she said.

"I had read about him in the Spiritualist Society newsletter. And then last month, I saw he was holding a public meeting in Brighton. Diana and I purchased tickets and took the train to see him."

As if on cue, Harry saw the door open, and Diana returned –
she, too, pulled out a chair and sat next to her aunt, taking her
hand again.

"And you were convinced?" said Kat after a minute.

"Oh yes. Enough to go back the next weekend. His *ability* was
remarkable. He made connections – for so many in the
audience."

"Did you speak to him privately?" said Harry.

"On the second occasion, yes."

"You sought him out?"

Harry watched Alice carefully as she pondered this question.

"No," said Alice. "Now that you mention it, I seem to
remember he approached us, after the meeting was over. Isn't
that right, Diana?"

"Yes, Aunt, I think so."

"Oh. He *knew* who you were?" said Harry, realising this could
be key.

"No. I don't believe so. He said he had seen me in the crowd
and somehow felt impelled to speak to me."

"I don't suppose you remember his *exact* words?" said Kat.

Harry saw Kat fire him a glance, the smallest of raised
eyebrows. Always a fetching look, to be sure, but in this case,
Harry knew Kat was signalling *that this might be important.*

Harry saw Alice frown, trying to recall. She looked at Diana
who shrugged, as if she couldn't remember either.

"Hmm, I think he said, 'Someone has a message for you, from
the other side'."

"And what did you do?"

"Well, I asked him who the message was from, of course, but
he said he couldn't be sure. It wasn't yet clear."

"Got it. So did he suggest maybe you should have a séance?"
said Kat.

"No, not at all. But we did begin a correspondence. A few
weeks later, he wrote that he had decided to set up some public
meetings in Mydworth, and so that's when I asked him if he might
be prepared to host a séance."

"The one at the Green Man last week?" said Harry.

"Yes. I went to that, and afterwards he suggested conducting a séance right here."

Before Harry could press further on this, he heard a knock at the door, and Lance entered with a tray of tea.

When they had all been served, Harry saw Diana nod dismissal to Lance, who frowned at her, as if weary of being ordered around again by Alice's niece, then left the room. Diana reached across and put her hand back on Alice's.

"Perhaps that's enough questions for now, Aunt Alice?" she said. "You mustn't overdo it."

"Only a couple more, then we'll be gone, I promise," said Kat, and Harry saw his wife put on her most persuasive smile.

Always works on me, he thought.

"Just a few minutes then," said Diana.

"The seating for the séance," said Kat. "I assume everyone's places were assigned beforehand?"

Alice was nodding before Kat had even finished.

"Oh yes, Bellamy decided where everyone should sit."

Kat nodded at this as Harry sipped his tea, watching and listening carefully.

"I guess," Kat said, "there was some system for that assignment? Some reason... who sat where?"

Harry saw Alice look away at that, thinking on the query.

"Well, I *imagine* so, but I didn't discuss that with Bellamy. I just helped to make sure everyone was in their correct place."

Harry saw Kat now scan the table, as if imagining the participants sitting there, the candles, the storm crashing into the room, the thunder and lightning adding to the eeriness.

A network of threads underneath, tugging at some kind of tapping mechanism...

"One final question, if you don't mind. How much did Mr Smythe charge you to hold the séance?"

"Charge me?"

Kat held a light smile in place, keeping this question light. When it might be anything but.

A DISTANT VOICE

"Charge? Why he didn't charge me anything at all!"

At that, Harry looked at Kat. Certainly not the answer he would have expected.

"But doesn't Mr Smythe expect to be paid for these private events?" he said. "A séance in someone's home?"

Alice's head bobbed in quick agreement.

"Oh, yes. A pretty penny too, I do believe."

"And yet," Harry said, "for this... no charge?"

"Well, you see, Sir Harry, Bellamy said he could see that I was of very limited means. I mean, *worse* than limited if I am being honest. And he said *that would not be problem at all!* That two of the other guests would be paying his usual fee, and that was simply fine. So generous of him, don't you think?"

Harry nodded at that.

Very generous, he thought. *But also — beyond curious. Suspicious.*

6.

A PLAN IS FORMED

KAT FELT THEY had gone as far as they could, and she nodded to Harry to steer things to a more amiable end – and an exit.

"I assume you will be going to Bellamy Smythe's Town Hall performance?" he said.

"Meeting," Alice corrected.

"Of course, yes, his *meeting* tonight."

"I shall. And there will be another séance, right here, tomorrow night. After all, I really didn't have the opportunity to spend much time with my dear father. Perhaps my brothers, too. And I have *so* many things to say; questions to ask."

"Will your sister be joining you too?" said Kat, realising that Alice and Diana had barely mentioned the girl's mother during the conversation.

The response was not what she expected.

She saw Alice's eyes dart quickly to the girl, who seemed to respond with the barest of shakes of her head.

"My sister and I," said Alice, slowly turning back to Kat, "let us say that we do *not* always see eye to eye on such matters as the spirit world."

Kat waited for Alice to say more. But the woman was not forthcoming.

"Well then, we will see you tonight," Harry said after a few seconds, his easy smile in place, making the air in the room lighter.

"Yes. Oh, should I have Lance show you out?"

"No need," Harry said. "I'm sure you have things to attend to."

Like the piles of shattered glass, thought Kat, as she took Harry's arm, and together they left the great room with its supposedly haunted table.

IN THE HALLWAY they said goodbye to Alice, and watched Diana gently lead her upstairs for a nap.

There was no sign of Lance, so they let themselves out, into the heat of the late morning, the sun so welcomingly bright after the gloom of the Grange.

Once out onto the little lane that led back to Mydworth, Harry took her arm.

"Well," he said. "I must say, that was interesting."

"Wasn't it just? Your thoughts?"

"To be honest—"

"Oh yes. Love when you turn *honest*—"

Harry grinned. "I'm feeling a tad peckish," he said. "How about we grab a bite of lunch first before we chat back home? Spot of – what's it called – cogitation?"

"Good idea. I have a phone call I want to make."

"Aha. Do you now? How very mysterious."

"Aren't I?" said Kat, enjoying teasing him.

As they approached the square, she heard the sound of some kind of rustic band playing, simple drums beating out a rhythm, a violin whipping up a chorus of exuberant voices.

"Sounds like the fun and games have started already," said Harry.

As he said that, Kat saw the most extraordinary sight emerging from the square onto Church Street: a long line of dancing, gyrating men, drums and bells in hand, wearing bizarre shirts and trousers festooned with green and white rags, like some crazed camouflage.

Even stranger, many wore lifesize paper and cloth horse's heads, garishly painted, mouths open, cardboard teeth bared.

The look – not fun at all – intimidating, strange. *Like something that had gone weirdly wrong with the circus.*

She turned to Harry.

"Let me guess," she said. "Not that I'm alarmed or anything, but this... just another local custom?"

"Indeed," he said. "Called hooden horses. Don't know any of the hoodeners personally. Completely harmless. Least, I think so."

Despite Harry's words and his light grin as the mad group came closer, she felt him steering her safely out of the way of the line of hoodeners as it jostled past.

Together they carried on up Church Street, avoiding the crowded square and the revels, to the Dower House for lunch.

WHEN THEY ENTERED, Maggie was there in the hallway, hat on, a sure signal that she was about to venture out of doors.

"Oh, *you two?* Didn't expect you back until the cocktail hour."

Kat smiled at Harry's longtime housekeeper; someone, she well knew, who had been so much more important in Harry's life than that title implied.

"Harry here is feeling a bit 'peckish'."

"Oh, my, well, I'm not sure what we have lingering in that refrigerator thing, I was just—"

Kat saw Harry hurry to the woman's side.

"No problem, Maggie dear. You carry on."

"I was just popping out to shop for dinner tonight."

"Good luck with that – the festivities have started already," said Harry. "What's on the bill of fare by the way?"

"Lamb chops with mint sauce, roast potatoes and my special carrots."

"Then, by all means, do carry on. I imagine Kat and I can organise something between said infernal fridge and the larder."

Kat saw Maggie nod at this. "I did boil up some eggs on the off chance. So—"

"There you are! Do we still have a jar of that delicious mayonnaise that Kat had shipped over from New York?"

"I believe we do."

Jolly good! Egg mayonnaise beckons! Any chance of some cress too?"

"If you venture into the herb garden. I should warn you though, Mr Jenkins is back there, trimming and tidying."

Kat had noticed – to the side of their house – a small buckboard (*not sure what they call it here*, she thought) and a sturdy, if sleepy-looking, horse in its traces, feedbag attached.

"Good old Jenkins. I shall check with him most politely."

Maggie gave Kat a smile as she passed, and then left to stroll down to the shops, perhaps meet up with some friends for afternoon tea and scones. Village life, with a great dinner to look forward to.

Harry came to her. "Meet you in the kitchen. I'm off to liberate some watercress."

KAT WATCHED AS her husband took a giant bite of the sandwich. Sometimes it seemed as if Harry might be back in his war years, quickly gobbling whatever was at hand, as fast as he could.

And, at least waiting until said bite had vanished, he said: "How's your egg mayonnaise, Lady Mortimer? As good as they make it back in New York?"

"You mean my *egg salad sandwich*?"

Harry laughed. "There, you see, not sure what happened to the colonies after our little disagreement. How is that," he pointed to the bright red ceramic bowl with the chopped eggs and mayonnaise, "in any way a 'salad'?"

And Kat thought about that and laughed. *He does, kind of, have a point.*

"So," said Harry, pouring them both a glass of water from a jug on the table, "where exactly are we?"

"Well," said Kat. "Bellamy Smythe must be – as we suspected – a con artist."

"Agreed. A clever one too. A free séance? He's playing Alice like a fly fisherman – controlling the lure expertly. Question is – why?"

"That I don't understand. Alice living in what seems near poverty? And her sister, too, by all accounts."

"Yes. Though we need to pay her a visit, to be sure of that."

"Agreed," said Kat.

"So just what is our fraudulent spiritualist up to?"

"Maybe simply raising publicity for his show at the Town Hall? That motive enough?"

"Possibly," said Harry. "Though there must be easier – and cheaper – ways to do that. All that planning with the fishing line? Pyrotechnics even!"

"So, what are we missing? He clearly sought Alice out in Brighton. But why?"

"You know, one thing did occur to me: whatever happened to all the Wetherby money?"

"Right. You said, back when you were a boy, the place looked well taken care of. Nicola did say they lost it all to 'death duties'. But is that really possible? The taxman took it all?"

"Oh, sadly *more* than just possible. Death duties, all that land taxed, buildings – yes, that's wiped out many estates around here."

"But wouldn't you have heard about it?" said Kat. "It would have been quite a big story? Especially if it rendered the survivors destitute?"

"You're right. But, well, I've been away all these years. Easy to miss. Maybe I should drop in on old Protheroe at the *Mydworth Mercury*? Been here since the dawn of time. Ask to check out their back issues?"

"Great idea," said Kat. "Who knows, he might even have something on Smythe."

Harry looked away, out of the open window, the midday sky cloudless. Then he turned back to her, took another bite of sandwich.

"By the way – saw you showing a lot of interest in just where everyone was seated for the séance?" he said.

"Yes. Trying to work out how Bellamy worked his table 'magic' without being spotted."

"Misdirection's the name of the game, I can tell you."

"Says the boy who dabbled in magic."

Harry laughed: "Must show you my Disappearing Ace trick sometime."

"To be sure. So, tell me about misdirection."

"Key bit of weaponry in the magician's arsenal. People will look where you direct them to look, missing things completely."

"And we know that there was a lot going on."

"Exactly. All the pulling on cables and wires could easily be missed."

Harry took a last bite, then wiped his hands on his napkin.

"What do you think about the nursery song?" said Kat.

"The fact that Smythe knew it?"

"Was a definite clincher for Alice."

"Indeed," said Harry. "Right now, I have absolutely no idea how he pulled it off. But I can guarantee he didn't get the song from the other side."

"I agree," said Kat, pushing her plate to one side. "So – this afternoon..."

"Need to track down Abel the barman. And the hairdresser, Mrs O'Connor. In fact, seems like we have quite a few people we need to talk to."

"Unfortunately, not Mr Bellamy."

"In splendid isolation in his rooms, as it were."

"How about we drop in on Christabel Taylor first? You notice Alice was a tad reluctant to talk about her?"

"Oh yes, definitely something frosty there," said Kat. "Diana too. By the way – I didn't ask – what are your thoughts on the girl?"

"Bit bouncy. Sweet. Clearly concerned about her aunt," said Harry. "Took her at face value, I'm afraid. Oh – you have that look."

"Look?"

"Quizzical. Or rather – unconvinced. You think I've missed something?"

Kat sipped at her glass of water. "I don't know. Now we're out of that strange house something's nagging me. Diana – the boy Lance – Alice… Just a sense that not everything is what it seems."

"Ah, well. You know me, Kat. I trust your instincts. Perhaps if we talk to Christabel we'll learn more."

He stood up, and Kat watched him take the plates over to the kitchen sink and start to wash them up.

"So, a trip to the sister," he said, looking over his shoulder. "And then we find this Maeve O'Connor, and pay a visit to Abel Coates at the Station Inn."

But Kat raised her hand, then got up to join him.

"Slightly *different* suggestion. You remember I said I needed to come back for the phone."

"Indeed. I shall be most interested to see *who* it is you call."

Kat, enjoying a secret almost as much as her husband, picked up a tea towel, gave him a kiss on the back of his neck and started to dry the dishes alongside him.

"Who knew dishwashing could be so thrilling," he said.

7.

THE MEDIUM'S GUESTS

HARRY PARKED THE Alvis outside Salon Maurice, and Kat quickly popped out of the car, engine still running.

"Okay," she said, leaning into the open window, "*you* go onto the Station Inn and find Abel Coates."

"Oh, going in here on your own then? I didn't—"

"I made an appointment. Figured, sitting in the chair, the woman would be kind of *stuck* answering my questions."

"Aha. So *that* was the secret phone call? Very clever."

"And believe I could use a little cut. Meet you back at the house?"

"For cocktails, before tonight's big show with Smythe?"

"Yes, and who knows" – she broadened her smile, loving teasing him like this – "maybe even a little R and R."

"R and R? You know, since we got married, that phrase has taken on a whole new meaning to me."

And with that, Kat turned – Harry's eyes still on her, she knew – and walked from the car and into Salon Maurice.

A MATRONLY LADY stood at a display cabinet, a small register nearby, beauty products on display under the glass.

"Hello," said Kat. "I have an appointment. Lady—"

The woman's face it up. "Oh, yes, Lady Mortimer."

Then Kat hurried to add: "With Mrs O'Connor. Just a bit of a trim."

At that, the manager of Salon Maurice, came out from behind the counter and – with all the grandness that she could summon – led Kat to a chair near the back, a pair of permanent wave machines lined up, electrical wires dangling ominously, and an unsuspecting Maeve O'Connor waiting with a smile.

ALTHOUGH IT COULDN'T be far off closing time, Harry saw – as he walked into the Station Inn, the room already smoky – that a sizeable crowd of regulars still stood at the bar, with the low rumble of weighty discussions of whatever, along with the occasional explosion of laughs.

Clearly, for many, the working day had ended early in anticipation of the festival weekend to come – and there was time for a lunchtime pint or two.

The Station wasn't a pub that Harry favoured much. Hard to find common ground with farm workers and men just off a building site, heavy boots showing the spattered signs of the day's work.

He walked to the side of the bar, out of the main fray, and stood, waiting for the barman to take notice of him, and walk over.

"What will it be, sir?" said the man.

"Pint of Best, if you wouldn't mind. Have one yourself?"

The barman grinned.

"Don't mind if I do, sir. You're a proper gentleman."

He grabbed a possibly clean glass from the counter behind him, then pulled on the tap to fill.

"I'll keep mine in the barrel, if that's okay with you, sir?"

"Of course," said Harry.

"Nice day for it," said the barman, easing the beer into the glass. "But then – every day's a nice day for it, that's what I say, eh?"

Harry laughed, going along with the banter. "How true!"

He had a good idea from Nicola's description that this was Abel Coates, and the jokey approach seemed to confirm that, but he needed to be sure.

"There you go, sir. Up to the brim, just as the good Lord intended!"

Then, as the barman put down the glass on the well-worn bar, Harry reached out, put down sixpence, slid it across the counter.

He raised the glass, took a mouthful.

"Cheers!" he said. And then began, "Abel, isn't it?"

The slightest of pauses. Then: "That's right, sir. Abel by name, able by nature!"

"Wonder if I could ask you a few questions about the other night?"

At first Coates didn't react, as if Harry might be looking into one of the rowdier nights at the bar, but then he said, "You know... at the Grange?"

Which didn't produce an answer.

But the question did have Coates fold his arms; a moment to think. Then, a sliver of a smile.

"No, sir. If you don't mind, you're not some kind of newspaper bloke are you? Because if you want my story, well *that'll* cost you a damn sight more than just a pint of ale."

"Not at all," said Harry, laughing. "No, I'm local. Just looking into things for a friend who was there."

He left the name of that friend – for now – hidden. Thinking: *Let him wonder about that.*

Coates recovered.

"I see," he said, contemplating Harry. And then, as if he'd come to a decision: "What is it you'd like to know, then?"

And a first hurdle passed, Harry took another sip of the cloudy beer, and started right at the most obvious question.

"Do you believe Bellamy Smythe really *can* talk to the spirit world?"

MAEVE O'CONNOR had kept her shears *clicking* and *clacking* and hadn't stopped talking about the séance since Kat had sat down in her chair.

Kat had originally planned to nudge the conversation gently around to the subject, but the chatty, gossipy hairdresser had leapt in straight away, excitedly asking if Kat had plans to see Smythe's show at the Town Hall.

Nothing the woman had said so far had contradicted Nicola's account of the séance though, and Kat was beginning to feel this might be a wasted hour.

Though the cut was certainly well above average.

Maybe I'll start coming here regularly, she thought.

"*Honestly,* I'll tell you, m'lady. I've never been so scared in all my life," the woman said, punctuating the conversation with a snip here, a snip there. "When I heard that voice! I swear it wasn't Mr Smythe speaking. He truly *was* possessed! And everything in that room – chaotic! The storm, the wind, the lightning!"

Kat was facing the mirror reflection of the two of them, the hairdresser clearly enjoying having such a tale to tell.

"You said that you were hoping to make contact with your own loved one again?"

"Ah, yes. My dear husband, Liam. Lost him at sea. Ship sunk—" another snip "—in 1918. I always felt like he was still somehow *here*, you know?"

"But he didn't make contact the other night?"

"No. Was a disappointment, I don't mind saying. Not my turn, I suppose. Still – he and I did speak together earlier in the week."

"Oh, at the Green Man, yes? I heard that Mr Smythe had held another séance."

"That's right. My lovely Liam, after all these years. He told me—"

Maeve paused her click-clacking – and Kat looked into the mirror. The hairdresser had a tear rolling down her cheek.

"Oh, I'm sorry," said Kat, suddenly remembering that people like Maeve, so desperate to believe, were gullible precisely because they were desperate. "We can talk about something else."

"No," said Maeve, wiping her eyes with a handkerchief for a moment, then picking up her scissors again. "It's *me* who should be sorry. Silly old me. Anyway, he told me he loved me very much, and for me to carry on being strong. And to keep making contact."

Of course, thought Kat. *He would say that, wouldn't he? Got to keep the cash rolling in.*

"That Mr Smythe," continued Maeve. "I'm so deeply grateful to him. *Such a wonderful man.*"

"He certainly sounds it," said Kat. "I suppose they must be very expensive, all these séances."

Was that a slight hesitation in the rhythmic clacking of the shears?

"Well, yes they can be. But you know, when the cost is shared with other participants, it's all very reasonable."

"Of course. I imagine at the Grange… quite a group."

"Exactly," said Maeve. "And, anyway, who can put a price on speaking to those you love who have departed?"

"Of course," said Kat.

That price — exactly what people like Bellamy Smythe depended on.

8.

CONVERTS

HARRY SAT WITH Abel at a corner table of the Station Inn, away from the crowd at the bar, his pint in front of him.

Abel had asked another of the staff to cover at the bar, when he realised Harry wanted to talk seriously, and when Harry hinted there might be a few quid in it for him.

Harry had pulled together a simple cover story: his 'old family friend' at the séance – Alice Wetherby – had been conned before, by another medium. And Harry just wanted to make sure that Bellamy Smythe wasn't up to the same tricks.

Abel nodded, seeming to understand that. He'd explained how he'd been dragged along to one of Bellamy's shows a couple of months back by a pal.

Said he'd expected the whole thing to be nonsense, and even heckled a few times from the audience.

But then Bellamy had picked him out of the crowd – and told him that his wife Betty had a message for him: *"put a sock in it, Abel, or you know what"* – that was the message.

And it was, word for word, what his dear, departed wife used to say to him when he'd had a few too many!

From that moment, he told Harry, he was a believer.

"There might be conmen around," the barman had said. *"But Bellamy Smythe ain't one of them."*

"SO, I'M CURIOUS – exactly how did you end up going to one of his séances?" said Harry, so far not hearing anything out of the ordinary.

"Funny that," said Abel. "When I saw he was doing one of his shows here in Mydworth, I went along to get a ticket. Thought maybe this time I'd get another chance to say hello to my Betty! Anyway, Mr Smythe is standing there with the ticket lady, and he just turns to me and says: 'Mr Coates, you don't want to talk to Betty in a big theatre. Come along to a séance. Do it properly.' Well, you could have knocked me down with a feather!"

Harry took a sip of his beer. So far, this sounded exactly the same *modus operandi* they'd heard from Alice.

And the way it worked – easy to figure.

Bellamy clearly does a bit of advance research on his audience, picks the ones he thinks might be ripe for plucking, pulls them right in.

"So you went along to the Green Man?" said Harry.

"That's right, Sir Harry. Bunch of other folk there – so we split the cost."

"And you made contact again?"

"No. Bit disappointing that was."

"Get your money back?" said Harry, smiling.

"Ha, no chance of that. He makes that clear up front!"

"Guess the spirit world can be a tad unpredictable? But you were still happy to go to the Grange, to another séance?"

"Oh yes," said Abel. "See, at the Green Man, there was other people came through from the 'other side'. That's what they call it, you know."

Harry nodded.

Abel leaned close, voice lowered.

"And proper scary it was. Table tapping – so loud! Then voices! Tell ya – Smythe was *gone*, taken over by someone else!"

Coates looked around as if recalling the moment. Took a sip of his beer.

Harry waited a moment.

"So, then, you were persuaded?"

"I was, yes. No doubt."

"And you don't think Bellamy might have been using – I don't know – some kind of clever deception?"

Harry saw Abel shrug.

"In truth? When I went to the Green Man – oh yes – I was looking out for that. You know – wires, accomplices, all the stuff you hear about con men using."

"But you didn't see anything?"

"Not a thing," said Abel, shaking his head.

"And at the Grange?"

"Same thing. I've been around a bit, you know? No one pulls the wool over Abel Coates's eyes! So when we went into that dining room, I pretended to drop my matches so I could have a good squint right under the table."

Harry didn't let it register that he had any added interest in what was to come.

Though, to be sure, he was very interested.

"But you didn't see anything?"

"Nah, not a bloody dicky bird. Just a lot of cobwebs and dust! That place is proper on the ropes!"

Harry laughed. But at the same time, he was thinking…

Could Bellamy really have concealed the wires so well? Or is Abel just goosing the story to make sure he gets his little tip?

"Abel, I'm wondering, are you going to the show tonight at the Town Hall?" said Harry.

"Oh, I'll be there, all right. I'm a 'convert', to be sure. That the right word?"

Harry smiled.

It wasn't the word he would use.

"NEARLY DONE NOW, Lady Mortimer," said Maeve, beginning to tidy up the final edges of Kat's trim.

The conversation had moved on from the séance at the Grange to village news, much of it now shared from customer to customer, the whole room at one point quite a babble – *who's seeing who, who's fallen out, who's up, who's down.*

A DISTANT VOICE

The hairdresser's more like a community centre for sharing the latest gossip.

But then Maeve leaned in closer to Kat, her eyes sympathetic.

"I was just thinking now, Lady Mortimer, all that time I was just blathering on about myself and my dear Liam."

"Not blathering, at all," said Kat, who was not at all sure what blathering even was.

"Selfish of me. I should have asked – is there nobody *you* have lost? Nobody you would wish to call out to?"

"Well, not really."

"No father or mother on the other side?"

"Both have passed," said Kat. "My mom died when I was a baby. And my dad – well, I imagine if they have bars in heaven, he'll be way too busy serving beers to want to chat to me."

Kat laughed – then, in the mirror she saw Maeve frown, as if she was somehow *disappointed* by her response. Or perhaps the woman was offended by her joke? But Maeve seemed to notice her looking and the frown quickly passed.

Time to change the subject, thought Kat.

"Been here long?" she said.

A hesitation. The initial answer, surprisingly evasive.

"A while. Yes."

That's odd, Kat thought. *In fact, it didn't sound like the truth.*

"How long?"

Kat saw Maeve glance quickly at the salon manager who was only yards away. She guessed that the hairdresser knew she'd have to answer truthfully.

"A little over a month. Wanted a change, I did. Mydworth – a nice little town, you know. Quiet. More like a village."

"Isn't it?" said Kat, now intrigued. "And where were you before you came here?"

"Oh, you know. All over."

"Not local?" said Kat, pressing now.

"No."

Kat wanted to keep pressing, this subject – for some reason – one that Maeve was uncomfortable with. But she saw the hairdresser put down her scissors and reach for a hand mirror. "There now! I think we're all done!" She held up the mirror for Kat to see. "What do you think?"

"Lovely," said Kat, surprised at the sudden finish, though pleased with the cut. Maeve clearly knew what she was doing. "I'll have to come back next month – ask for you *personally*."

"Very kind of you."

"If you're still here, of course," said Kat, smiling.

She watched Maeve carefully. The woman smiled back. But, in her eyes, there was something else.

Not humour.

But a cold look.

Even, perhaps, a calculating look.

And Kat had to wonder, *why should Maeve O'Connor be so sensitive to being questioned about where she had moved from?*

Unless...

She was deliberately hiding something.

HARRY DROVE BACK to the Dower House. Kat would soon be back from the salon, a pleasant walk away.

As he passed the square, he saw another group of Morris dancers performing outside the King's Arms – a boozy crowd watching.

Whatever would Kat make of some of these Midsummer performers – if you could call them that – who were now beginning to pop up all around the village?

His American wife had shown herself quite adaptable to English village life, with its unspoken rules and quirky customs.

But these mad Midsummer events already in progress?

He wondered what she had learned at Salon Maurice? His own one-man jury was still out on Abel Coates.

He'd slipped the man a pound note at the end of their chat. But, in truth, he felt perhaps he'd been robbed. Abel liked the sound of his own voice, and Harry suspected that all he had heard should perhaps have been taken with a pinch of salt.

Especially the nonsense about checking under the table.

If Harry was right – and Bellamy *had* used a cable rig – then it would have been clearly visible to anybody who'd put their head under there.

Had Abel really looked? Or had he just invented that to appear to be a man of the world?

"Nobody fools old Abel Coates?"

Indeed!

But, Harry thought, *there could be another explanation.*

What if Abel was working for Bellamy? What if absolutely everything he'd said at the pub was just a clever charade to deflect Harry's interest?

It seemed almost outlandish. Nevertheless, he made a mental note to – somehow – add a background check of Abel Coates to their to-do list.

Still, he thought, as he reached the top of School Lane and turned to drive past the church, there were opportunities to learn more this evening. Bellamy Smythe's demonstration at the Town Hall – standing room only, Harry had heard. The man himself should be more easily cornered there.

And maybe – if he could grab half an hour at the *Mydworth Mercury* archive tomorrow – he'd learn more about what had happened to the Wetherby estate?

Could the entire inheritance really have all been swallowed up in death duties?

He stopped the car near the front door. A steady plume of thin smoke from the chimney showed that Maggie was back, dinner being prepared.

Cocktail hour approaching. Then, after what would definitely be delicious roast lamb and mint sauce, off to the Town Hall.

To finally see Bellamy Smythe in action.

Harry doubted that the demonstration, if that's what it must be called, would impress him at all.

But, on that score, he would learn that he was entirely *wrong*.

9.

SHOWTIME AT MYDWORTH TOWN HALL

KAT WATCHED AS Harry took his seat next to his aunt Lavinia, nodding and smiling to others nearby in the audience. Then she joined them in the row, sitting to Harry's right.

Lavinia – surprisingly – looked as if she was actually comfortable sitting at the heart of this packed house, in spite of the hard and unforgiving foldaway chairs.

Harry had telephoned Lavinia barely an hour before, to see if she knew anything at all about the Wetherbys, and their descent into poverty.

But though she had a faint recollection of some rumoured mystery surrounding the estate, after so many years she couldn't recall the details – if there were any – and agreed the *Mydworth Mercury* was the place to go.

Then, when Harry had mentioned the Town Hall demonstration, she informed him that she, too, most *definitely* wanted to go, *wouldn't miss it for the world*. Fortunately, Nicola was able to secure a last-minute ticket to the sold-out event.

As soon as Kat joined her, Lavinia leaned across Harry and whispered to her.

"I never suspected that there'd be *this* many gullible people in all of Mydworth."

It had been intended as a whisper, but with Lavinia's voice raised to be heard above the hub-bub, Kat was sure some of those nearby described as "gullible" had heard the appellation.

Harry kept a steady smile on his face, then, as he gave Kat a quick glance, a roll of his eyes. His aunt's occasional bluntness – she knew – he had learned to live with.

Kat looked around the crowded Town Hall: it took her right back to the rough and ready theatres of New York's Tenderloin, and their somewhat glitzier relatives up on Broadway.

A lifetime ago, she thought.

Harry was looking at his aunt, who was still leaning across him.

"You know, Aunt Lavinia, we *could* swap seats if you'd like to do a running commentary for Kat."

Lavinia, not one to miss the message, looked up, smiling. "I am perfectly fine *right here*, Harry. Just curious to discover what we shall see that warrants... *this.*" And she gave a wave at the filled rows to the front and back of them.

"I must say," Harry said, as he looked from his aunt then to Kat, "I'm curious about that too. Now, if this was a Houdini kind of fellow, complete with vanishing elephants and inescapable locked chests, well then I could see the excitement."

"Guess whatever Bellamy Smythe does," Kat said, "it must be quite *something.*"

"Ah, but what exactly?" Harry mustered. "Oh look, some familiar faces."

Kat turned in the direction of Harry's gaze, where she saw some regulars from the village that she had come to know amid the sea of people.

BUT HARRY HAD also spotted someone that Kat didn't know.

"See the chap there, just removing his bowler? Abel Coates. Attended the séance."

"Never understood those things at all!" Lavinia said.

For a moment Kat thought Lavinia was referring to Coates's choice of hat.

"I mean, all that effort to speak to the departed when, in my experience, people probably had little desire to speak to them when they were alive and kicking."

"Excellent point, Aunt."

Kat had to admit, she loved listening to Harry and his aunt discuss just about *anything*. As if their conversation was a fast-paced parlour game.

"And I see my new favourite hairdresser," she said.

Lavinia turned to comment on that. "Now that *does* interest me! I absolutely adore that cut, Kat. Very modern!"

"She's over there," said Kat, pointing discreetly. "Maeve O'Connor, from Salon Maurice. Another séance attendee, and from what I learned today, a devotee of Smythe."

Maeve O'Connor sat to one side, a few rows in front of Abel Coates. Not talking to anyone.

Which, Kat guessed, made sense. New here, not really knowing anyone. Though quite the chatterbox during today's haircut.

She turned and saw Harry still craning around, looking at the room. Being "Sir Harry" of Mydworth Manor, she knew he had to nod and smile at people who knew him, while he most likely didn't have the foggiest idea who they were.

"Oh, looks like the Wetherbys have arrived," he said.

Kat turned to the rear and saw Alice walking in, with her niece Diana at her side. Her face beamed with a big smile – eyes looking excited. Definitely a convinced acolyte.

Or, as Lavinia might say, *one of the most gullible.*

"No sign of the sister, Christabel, though," said Kat, as Alice and Diana took the last two seats in one of the rows at the front. "Least as far as I can tell."

"Generally, you don't see them together much, that I *do* know," said Lavinia. "Oil and water, or so I have been told by the ever-knowledgeable Mr Benton back at the house. But sharing one thing."

"What is that?" Kat said.

"Poor as church mice, barely hanging on, the two of them."

Harry nodded at that, then, his voice low.

"We're going to try and speak to her tomorrow." He turned to his aunt, leaned close, but Kat could still also hear. "Christabel was also at the séance when the dear old Major made his 'appearance'."

"The father?" said Lavinia. "I do believe I met him once, you know. Not the *warmest* of men, I must say. Rather – what's the kindest word – stern, strict. *Victorian.* And..." Now Lavinia lowered her voice. "*Clearly* favoured the sons over his daughters."

Kat scanned the room again, thinking, *Must be half of Mydworth crammed into the hall.*

Until, with no discernible cue, the steady noise of the crowd, chatting away as people do before a show, started to quieten. All perhaps sensing that the moment was soon at hand.

Lower still.

The house lights began to dim. This was no fancy West End theatre, Kat knew, but it was still quite effective.

The audience was consumed in a murky darkness – the stage curtain catching the only light.

Everyone waited. As if some amazing spectacle was about to be revealed.

A few moments more, and the curtain parted just a few feet.

Out walked what had to be the source of all this attention, in cutaway tuxedo and black pants: *Bellamy Smythe himself.*

Despite having done absolutely nothing so far – his reputation obviously preceding him – the audience began applauding.

Kat reached across – because it seemed like a natural thing to do, in a theatre, at a show – and clasped Harry's right hand.

And Bellamy's voice, clear, strong – matched with the man's piercing blue eyes, visible even from here – rang out.

"GOOD FRIENDS AND neighbours, welcome to what I promise you will be a *very special evening.*"

Kat saw Smythe smile at that, looking so reassuring as if dabbling with spirits and such was nothing at all to be alarmed about.

"Many of you will be visited tonight by dear ones that you have not heard from in such a long time. Some of you will relive moments from the past, forgotten, even hidden. But now, for a brief hour" – Smythe spread out his arms as if embracing the entire crowd – "you good people of Mydworth, with all your disparate hopes, your fears, your memories and loss – are intimately joined *together*."

Smythe pulled his arms back to his side as if hauling in a net full of eager fish – the audience, Kat felt, were already his.

"First, the *quickest* of demonstrations – an amusement, if you will. Each of you think of a number, between one and fifty. Yes? But…" Smythe raised a finger as if in warning, Kat was already searching for an appropriate number in her own head. "*That* number must, of course, be an odd number, and you must not repeat any of the two digits." A smile as if that last injunction was obvious. "For example, you *cannot* select the number 11! Go on, each and every one of you, free of choice, select your number." He paused. "Do you have it?"

He waited, and Kat had to admit – not sure whether it was the presentation or the electric air of the crowd – she felt excitement.

"*Good.* You see, I, too, have that number you selected."

He smiled again, keeping this all so light. "Right *here*."

And Smythe touched the outside pocket of his tuxedo, and slipped out a piece of paper, folded in half.

He looked at it first, grinning as he did, before slowly turning and showing the crowd the number written down, boldly, in thick black ink.

"All of us *are* together tonight, you see, since you all have picked *this* very number, yes?"

Kat had selected the number thirty-five.

And her mouth fell open when Smythe showed the large "3" and "5" on the piece of paper.

The crowd was suddenly buzzing and mumbling in clear astonishment.

She quickly turned to her husband.

"Harry, did you—"

And he leaned into her, squeezing her hand back gently as he did.

"Of course. *Kind* of know how that was done. Not bad, I must say – though I think he may have to raise the bar to really impress this crowd. Or me at least."

And when the audience stopped responding to this seemingly amazing feat performed by Smythe, *raising the bar is exactly what he did.*

Kat watched him step forward to the very edge of the stage, then raise his hands – still clasping the piece of paper, his face now serious, those eyes mesmerising, icy – until the crowd went silent.

In the silence, he tore the paper into smaller and smaller pieces, then let them go, the fragments fluttering to the floor at the feet of the tightly-crammed front row.

"What do you think you *saw* just now, ladies and gentlemen?" said Bellamy, his gaze slowly scanning the whole room. "I shall tell you."

He turned, strode to the back of the stage, then turned again and shook his head dramatically.

"Nothing but a cheap trick. A psychological manipulation. A simple 'effect' that even a children's entertainer might master."

Kat felt the Town Hall go silent now, this speech so unexpected.

"If you came here tonight, expecting to see more such tricks, then I am afraid you will be disappointed. In fact – I suggest you leave now." He raised his voice, until it echoed from the rear of the hall, and pointed to the exit doors. "Yes! Do you hear me? Leave now! There will be nothing tawdry like that for you here!"

The audience froze in their seats as Bellamy dropped his arm, scanning the hall, as if daring people to go. Then he walked slowly to the front of the stage again, and crouched down, his voice dropping almost to a whisper.

"Because *you*..." And now he raised a finger and pointed slowly, one by one at wide-eyed faces across the room, his voice hoarse. "*You* – *you* – and *you* – in fact, all of us..." He opened his hands wide now, palms up, and slowly stood. "*Yes, all of us* are going to bear witness to spirits crossing the threshold tonight. Piercing the veil that separates the living from the undead, as many of you will hear the words of your beloved ones."

As he said those words, in spite of herself, Kat felt a shiver run through her bones, and guessed she was not the only one in the hall to do so.

If nothing else, Smythe was certainly an effective showman.

A DISTANT VOICE

10.

VOICES FROM THE PAST

HARRY LOOKED AT a woman, a few rows ahead, standing up. The audience's eyes locked on her, and on – yards away at the edge of the stage – a very serious Bellamy Smythe.

The woman had shrieked and stood up when Bellamy mentioned that there was someone here, tonight, whose son had gone missing years ago. Someone who loved his football, his pals – and yet – had mysteriously disappeared.

Only to be found, hundreds of miles away on a street in Liverpool. The fatal victim of some terrible crime.

Smythe nodded so seriously as he spoke, turning away as if shielding those strong blue eyes from the audience.

"He needs you to know... he has not forgotten you. And he knows... that you keep his room exactly as it was."

The woman worked a small kerchief in her hands, hanging on every word.

"He says he can *even* see that you have kept his wardrobe *just as it was*. His school uniform, still hanging there." Smythe smiled. "The adventure books he loved... that *you* gave him."

The woman, Harry saw, was nodding at every word.

Then Smythe finally turned back to her. "Your son asks that you... yes... *donate* those books to the village library, in his name." The woman's head nodded. "And lastly, he says... he loves you."

And at that, Smythe did something quite clever, Harry thought. After all, he had a large audience to "work" and couldn't stick with one person for *too* long. It was a move one might see a vicar use to calm an agitated flock.

Hands out, he signalled that this moment of "contact" was at an end.

The woman seemed to understood that, slowly sitting down, while her neighbours comforted her with gentle touches to her arms and her agitated hands.

Clever, thought Harry. *Has a lot of information – picked up from somewhere.*

A murmur of conversation bubbled up in the audience, and Harry saw Bellamy raise one hand to his temple, as if a particularly difficult message was now coming through. He held one hand out, requesting silence again.

The audience obeyed.

"So *many* voices," said Bellamy. "But wait – one *louder,* insistent. Ah yes. A father with another word for his 'bonny girl'."

At this, Harry spun round to Kat, seeing that she, too, had recognised the code – then he peered across the rows at Alice Wetherby – one hand steadying herself on the back of the chair in front, the other pressed tightly against her mouth.

Bellamy didn't look directly at Alice – instead, staring down at the stage. "We shall speak… tomorrow, he says. No… he *insists.* There is something he must tell you. Something you must do – so that he may at last be allowed to move on."

Bellamy stood up, shaking his head as if to clear it.

Harry saw him steal the barest of glances at Alice in the audience, and give her a discrete nod.

And then, as if shooting metaphysical ducks in a barrel, he went onto others in attendance, half a dozen more departed "spirits" had entered the theatre, all eager to have their say.

Until something happened that Harry didn't expect at all.

As his own past suddenly began to appear in the room as well.

HARRY WATCHED AS Smythe turned from the audience, and suddenly wrapped his arms around himself, as if… *shivering.*

A DISTANT VOICE

Then his voice took on a deep, hollow sound.

"*It is night.* And oh-so-cold. Everyone, *so* cold. They shouldn't be out here, but they are. And someone is right here, with us now, and yet, years ago, there too."

Harry shifted in his seat.

"Everyone looks not at the great ship's still-glittering interiors – but out to the dark, moonless sea. To small waiting boats. People yelling, scrambling, some boats already lowered into that icy sea, and, and—"

Bellamy turned slowly to look out at the audience.

"No, it's a mere boy. *Waiting.* Someone holds his hand. But not his mother. His father. As, yes, his father leans close, and says... '*You must go. Leave this ship now with,*'" a dramatic pause, "'*Maggie.*'"

Harry felt Kat squeeze his hand. Without taking his eyes off Bellamy he could tell that Lavinia had also turned to look straight at him.

Harry made his breathing steady. A little trick of control he'd learned when things got dicey up the air, during the war. *Just breathe through it,* his CO had told him. *One breath at a time.*

"Then... the mother close. The father telling him, 'We will be with you so soon...' as they quickly hug and release that boy to get into one of those terrible boats. And, and..."

Bloody hell, Harry thought as the stage light actually picked up a glimmering of a teardrop in the man's right eye.

The bastard.

"And then" – Bellamy himself took a deep breath, bringing the audience to that moment – "the boy steps into the boat. The boat lowers, into the cold sea, away from the great sinking ship."

Smythe stopped as a warm smile crept onto his face.

"They are here now. They need *you* to know that they love you. And always will – even though that boy... is no longer a boy."

Harry could feel the looks from some in the audience, those who knew of this seldom-shared story. Those villagers who were around in 1912, when the great Titanic had slid into its deep and icy grave.

Lavinia leaned into him.

"Steady, Harry. Right?"

Harry kept his face placid, hiding his rage at this spectacle being staged by Smythe.

"Oh, yes. *Nice and steady*. Of course."

He turned to his wife, whose face showed that she shared every disturbing feeling that this "performance" of Bellamy Smythe's had summoned.

"If I didn't have to interview the charlatan, I'd go up there now and rip him right in two. But that" – he smiled, eager to show both Lavinia and Kat that he was, indeed, under control – "can wait for later."

And in moments, Smythe moved on to yet more displays of spirits descending on the Mydworth Town Hall.

While he and Kat waited to confront him at show's end.

AS THE PLEASED and impressed audience – chattering away – began to file out, Harry led Kat to a small staircase up to a door, stage left, that opened onto the back stage and what passed as dressing rooms.

Lavinia had set out for the front, where Benton would be waiting in the Rolls.

In seconds they were at an open door where Bellamy Smythe was undoing his black tie, and had removed his tuxedo. A nearby back door would complete his escape.

But not this time.

"Mr Smythe," Harry said, "we'd like a word, if you don't mind."

Then, with the two of them literally blocking Bellamy Smythe's way out, Harry began the interrogation without waiting for an answer.

KAT COULDN'T IMAGINE what Harry had felt, with his own horrific experience being used as part of the tawdry spirit show. But she knew he was a man who was used to controlling things – starting with his own emotions.

Smythe appeared almost pleased to see them, as if his summoning of a night Harry would never forget had – for him – had the desired effect.

"Yes – I can talk with you, a few moments. Very weary after such an event. Quite something, this evening."

She saw Harry take a step towards the man, tightly closing the distance between the two of them.

"Yes, all *very* impressive. At some point we must have a chat about how you find those little titbits you use to create your make-believe spirits. But I must say, tonight—"

Smythe's face registered that his performance had done anything but win over Sir Harry.

"—you seem to have gotten one small detail *wrong*, you see."

"Sometimes, the spirit world—"

Harry shot up a hand, cutting Smythe off.

Though it looked to Kat as if he could easily punch the man in the face.

"That night you were talking about? The cold. The dark sea? One very important detail you got wrong. I imagine you made your best guess. But no, you got it terribly wrong."

Now it was Smythe who was confused.

"My father did indeed talk to me, in those last moments."

Harry looked at Kat. He had hardly ever talked to her about that experience, all those years ago. How Maggie, his housemaid turned guardian, had gotten into the lifeboat with him.

"You see, Smythe, my father held my hand tight for a few moments and said – his voice so very low so my mother would not hear – 'Son, I always want you to know the truth. The truth is such an important thing. And *you* must go. Your mother insists on staying with me. But, we may not make it.'"

Harry stopped. His words, Kat felt, even more chilling than Smythe's performance on stage.

"Of course, he cried then, while still urging me to move away, my mother's maid gently tugging. *That* – is what really happened. Too bad your spirits somehow got it wrong. Probably because they are as full of *bull* as you are."

"Sir Harry, I did not mean—"

Wondrously, Kat saw Harry shift, relaxing, even a bit of a smile on his face.

"Now then, as I said, we do have some questions for you. Before you dash away."

And Harry turned to Kat, as if this backstage conversation had never happened.

"MR SMYTHE," KAT began, "we've spoken with Alice Wetherby, and she described how she went to see you, more than once, and how you then... sought her out."

At that, Smythe didn't say anything. His face rigid, probably unsure where this might be going.

"Which led to the two recent séances, oh – and the one to come tomorrow night." Kat paused. "Can you tell us exactly *why* you approached her?"

She saw Smythe's eyes dart right as if wishing there was a back exit from the room.

"Go on, old man," Harry said. "Cards on the table, as it were."

Then Harry dropped a sly reference that probably unsettled Smythe even more.

"After all, your performance tonight, what you do – we can easily see all the hidden wires and strings, eh?"

Smythe was biding his time, searching for an answer.

"Why did I approach her? Because I could see, deep in her eyes, such a yearning to reach out to the other side."

"Oh, here we go," Harry said.

Kat pressed on. "So out of *all* the people who come to your... *performances*... you picked her as someone to contact personally?"

A quick nod. "I did. You two may not believe this but I have... unusual sensitivities."

"I *bet*," Harry added.

"I can tell people who are suffering. Sense what they seek. I recognise those who will benefit from a more *private* session with me, a select séance, to reach their departed loved ones. That is all."

Kat saw Smythe, having been initially knocked off his feet some, now slowly regaining his confidence.

"Quite the show, we heard," Harry said.

Smythe looked from Harry to Kat. "If you know what happened that night, you know that a true manifestation occurred. And you also know – I charged the poor woman *not a penny.*"

Kat nodded as he said that.

"Yes, she told us that. Which is why we wondered what's in it for you?"

Smythe smiled, as if he now had their measure.

"You think I do this for *money*? No. Alice Wetherby was desperate. I was moved to help her."

Kat doubted very much this charlatan could really be moved by *anything.*

"Now, I must return to my rooms. And I must say, if you persist in pestering me, I shall be forced to summon the police."

"Well, that is one thing you *might* actually be able to summon," Harry said.

Kat had to smile at that. This game with Harry? *Always more than fun.*

She started to step away from the cornered man but then – calculated, planned – turned back to him.

"If your motives are so – *innocent*," she said, "then perhaps you'll allow one of us to attend the séance with Alice tomorrow night?"

"What? Absolutely *not*. That will be a very special session. Outsiders *cannot* be part of it."

Kat nodded, guessing that would be the answer.

"Makes perfect sense," said Harry. "Outsiders can be *so* disruptive, can't they?"

Harry turned to leave the room, and she followed his cue.

But then he paused and added: "Do be careful out there, Mr Smythe. Midsummer revels are in full swing. Oh, and *lots* of spirits of a different kind as well."

Then he walked out, Kat stifling a laugh as she followed.

AS THEY EMERGED into Market Square, they were caught up instantly in a mad mix of dancers, men in horse heads, a band of pipes and horns caterwauling on the nearby stage, flaring torches adding to the strangeness.

Kat took Harry's arm as they walked.

"If it's like this tonight, what will it be like tomorrow?" she said.

"Oh, it's just the usual Midsummer high jinks," said Harry.

"You participate?"

"Haven't done for years. Gave up wearing papier-mâché horse heads *long ago*. But I'll tell you one thing, Kat, nothing beats a midnight trek up Myers Hill followed by a jolly good dance round a bonfire of pagan effigies."

"Pagan effigies? I'm afraid we don't have them where I come from, so I'll take your word for it."

Harry laughed as they ducked through a line of dancers and reached the edge of the crowd.

"So, Lady Mortimer," he said. "It's late — and I am overdue for a whisky at home — but thoughts on Mr Smythe?"

"Okay. He's after something from Alice, all right. Has to be money, no?"

"That would make the most sense, forgetting all that nonsense about his 'sensitivity'."

"We need to see Christabel in the morning. See what she knows."

"Yes. And your idea, to check the newspaper archives? That too."

They turned into the narrow, cobbled High Street that led home, the sound of bells and banging of drums, the laughing and shouts from the Midsummer revellers, fading away behind them.

"I was looking for an accomplice in the audience, but I didn't see anyone," said Kat, as they passed the Green Man and crossed Church Lane. "Did you?"

"No. But he must have one. Someone trawled Mydworth for all that information he used."

"Remember I told you Maeve O'Connor got edgy when I asked her how long she'd been in town?"

"Hmm. The hairdresser? Perfect profession to pick up boatloads of gossip. Ask innocent questions. Family histories and so on. Then feed it all back to Smythe."

"I'll check her out tomorrow. See what I can find."

They turned into the drive that led round behind the church towards the Dower House.

"I just wish we could somehow be there, tomorrow evening."

"Yes? There?"

"At the séance," Kat said.

And at that, Harry stopped, turned to her. The moon low in the sky.

He gave her a slow kiss.

"You know, I think… I *just* might be able to help you with that," he said.

And then without revealing how he would pull *that* off, he turned as they continued on their way home.

11.

A MORGUE AND A MAUSOLEUM

HARRY SQUINTED IN the sunlight. Kat was dressed in a simple summery dress, blue and white stripes. With the backdrop of the Dower House and the front garden, she could be posing for a magazine cover.

"Right, okay," he said. "I'd better be off, not sure what I will find in the archive."

"*Morgue.*"

"Sorry?"

"There are a lot of newspapers in New York City, and those old issues can often be very useful. But they don't call the place an 'archive'."

"No?"

"No. Called the 'morgue'."

"I see. For dead papers, dead stories."

He watched Kat turn and start for the wrong side of the car to drive before, stopping, grinning, and coming back to the right side.

"Old habits," she said. "Oh, and yes… sometimes those dead stories… not so dead."

"I will keep that in mind. Catch up later? After your little chat with Alice's sister."

"And remember, you were going to reveal to me how we might attend tonight's séance?"

"Oh yes. Haven't forgotten that."

He watched his wife slip into the Alvis, start the engine and spin the car around with a speed that he could only describe as *"quite American"*.

Then he popped his panama on his head and strolled down the drive into Mydworth.

AT FIRST GLANCE, Kat thought she must have the wrong address for Christabel Taylor's house. The tiny front garden was just two drab square patches, a misshaped crab apple tree in need of trimming, and the house looked barely more than a humble cottage.

She felt tentative about knocking, but then rapped hard on the wooden door.

After a second series of sharp knocks, a click as the door opened, and there was Diana, Christabel's daughter, eyes wide, clearly surprised by the visit.

"Oh, hello – I, er was just..."

"Diana – sorry for dropping by. But was hoping to speak with your mother. Is she—"

"Here? No." Then a bit of a smile crossed the girl's face. "She's off talking to Granpa, you see."

And Kat immediately thought: *is Christabel also buying into the idea of voices from the beyond?*

But Diana's smile broadened. "Oh, *not* what you're thinking. She's up at the family mausoleum. Most days she goes there. Prays. Always seems to feel better when she comes back."

"You think it's okay if I go see her there?"

"Why not?"

"And the mausoleum... where would I—?"

Diana waved a hand in the direction off a wooded hill to her left. "It's at the bottom of Myers Hill, behind the Grange. There's a path from here – easier than driving. Can't miss it. Just follow the path through the wood."

"Thank you."

As Kat turned, Diana said, "You and Sir Harry… helping my aunt. I appreciate it. Thank you."

"Not at all."

"You haven't uncovered anything… anything *bad*, have you?"

And despite the suspicions she and Harry had, Kat smiled and said, "No, nothing yet. Don't you worry."

She then turned on her way to the woods, the mausoleum and the resting place of Major Arthur Wetherby.

HARRY SAT AT a long table in the dingy archive room of the *Mydworth Mercury* and reached out for another of the heavy, leather binders that the young assistant had retrieved for him.

He checked the spine. On each binder, a year was stamped in faded gold.

He'd started with 1914, and found a few mentions of Major Wetherby – a couple of rousing, patriotic letters to the editor, even a photograph of the Major at a dinner of the Royal Sussex Regiment in Chichester.

Then he found a story about his renovation of the Wetherby Mausoleum – just months before the outbreak of war – the Major speaking of it as a tribute to his ancestors that was long overdue.

With the article, Harry saw a photograph of the stonemasons, all standing proudly in front of the building, the Major shaking someone's hand.

Harry thought how ironic this was, given the deadly impact that the war was so soon to have upon the family.

But apart from these stories, he found nothing about war service, or the Major's two sons.

At least there was no distraction to his researches in here. By Saturday morning, the weekly edition was already printed and out on sale. The great, black linotype machine (pride of the ancient editor, Bill Protheroe), visible through a wall of windows behind him, stood silent.

Just the assistant in the main office, sweeping up, filing, preparing for Monday, when this place would again be a busy, chattering blizzard of paper, thick with pipe and cigarette smoke. Harry opened the binder, the leather creaking as he lay it flat, and began to work his way through the pages. January, 1915. An English ship lost… Fighting on the border with Greece… Zeppelin raids in the Home Counties.

And, for a few seconds, he was a boy again, devouring these very pages, seeking tales of derring-do, innocent of the real cost of war which – within just a few years – he would himself know, so well.

KAT'S WALK ON the trail quickly turned into rather a gloomy one for such a sunny morning. The trees, close together, were old and thick as if eager to reclaim the well-trodden dirt path. Soon, the trees and bushes were so dense that she couldn't even see the nearby Grange.

For a moment, she wondered if she had perhaps selected the wrong trail. One thing she had noticed was that the English took the giving of directions quite lightly, with all sorts of not-very-helpful directives such as, *"well you just head down that way a bit, till you see a turning or two"*.

She guessed this trail would eventually lead to up to Myers Hill, one of the highest points in the area.

Then, just as she began to doubt that she was on the *right* path, the trail opened up to an area where the trees had been cut back; a small clearing.

At the far end of the clearing, she saw a stone mausoleum, an imposing colonnaded structure, with a pyramid shape for a roof, pointing straight to the heavens – the tomb much bigger than she might have imagined.

Flanking the entrance – atop the nearest left and right column – kneeling angels watched over it all.

A metal door stood *wide open*. From here, looking pitch dark inside.

Someone clearly had opened it, and was inside.

The setting, all alone here on the hill, was somewhat disturbing. She thought, last time she had seen such a tomb was at Saint Raymond's Cemetery in the Bronx, when she watched her own mother lowered into a simple dirt grave.

She slowed her pace as she approached.

If it was me inside there, she thought, *the last thing I'd want someone to do would be to rush in and scare me to death.*

FINALLY – HAVING WORKED his way laboriously through the binder – Harry found news of the Wetherby tragedy: the deaths of Major Wetherby and his two sons.

Victims of the Great Push of October 1915, the Royal Sussex suffering heavy casualties. The Major hit by a shell burst at company HQ behind the lines. Just a day later, his two sons lost in the futile infantry attack on the flat desolate battlefield of Loos, in Northern France.

Brave, yes. But all of it… such a waste, Harry thought.

The first news story just a brief notice of 'Missing in Action'. Then – days later – the deaths confirmed, followed within weeks by an obituary for the Major, as befitting this "Heroic son of Mydworth" as the paper called him at the time.

Harry moved quickly on to 1916, looking for the details of any wills and the estate. Finally, he found it: each of the three family deaths, in order, showing significant death duties, the estate dwindling, until barely anything remained to be passed on to the two daughters, Christabel and Alice.

He jotted down the grim figures on his notebook, then sat back to examine them, puzzled.

Something not quite right. The value of the estate to begin with, was much lower than he might have expected from such a family.

"Now here's a face I don't see often enough," came a familiar voice behind him.

Harry turned, to see Bill Protheroe, the bearded, pipe-smoking editor, at the door of the archive room, bearing two steaming mugs.

A DISTANT VOICE

"Bill," said Harry. "You not playing cricket today?"

"Midsummer Festival," said Bill, pulling up a chair and joining him. "Can never get a team together. Leastways – during this nonsense – not a sober one."

"Don't forget, if you're ever short of players, just give me a call, old boy."

"And deprive your beautiful wife of your company on a Saturday? She'd never forgive me!"

"Oh, Kat has a very forgiving nature," said Harry, taking one of the mugs of tea. "Cheers."

"Cheers," said Bill, leaning over to look at the binder. "And what are you up to... digging in the ancient pages of 'Hatch, Match and Despatch'?"

Harry laughed at the reference to Births, Marriages and Deaths.

"The estate of Major Arthur Wetherby, deceased, October 1915. Funny – it appears to be rather lighter on cash assets than I would have expected."

"Really? You're surprised? Ah, but – of course, I forget. You were but a mere boy at the time. Far too young to be aware... of the rumours."

"Yes – still a lad, back then. Perhaps you can tell me now about the rumours – not a trace of them in here."

Bill raised his eyebrows, feigning shock.

"Oh, you won't find rumours in the *Mydworth Mercury*. Paper of record, old chap."

Harry laughed. "Wouldn't have it any other way. But – though it may not be in the paper – I'd put money on you knowing all about it, Bill. So how about it? Between us? Out with it."

"Well," said Bill, putting down his mug, "if you insist. But you didn't hear this from me. Agreed?"

"Agreed."

And Harry listened, while Bill Protheroe revealed the true story of the Wetherby estate.

12.

VOICES FROM THE PAST

KAT TOOK A step into the darkness, the air suddenly cold, and as her eyes slowly adjusted to the gloom, she could make out shapes. The space was circular – just two small opaque windows high up in the whitewashed wall.

Directly ahead of her, towering over the space, was a marble crest, all angels and shields, a stone sword at its heart.

Beneath it, set into the wall, a series of carved slots for the stone coffins, maybe a dozen of them, some of them filled – but two or three still empty.

Those empty spaces, she thought, *awaiting the next generation of Wetherbys.*

High above, carved deep into the stone, and running all around the circular room, were words in Latin. She recognised them from the portrait of the Wetherbys she'd noticed back at the Grange.

And deep inside the mausoleum, ahead of her, Kat saw a stone pew, and someone kneeling, their back to the entrance.

Christabel Taylor, she guessed.

The woman had not heard her enter, which made this even harder to do.

"Christabel," Kat said, as gently as she could.

And she saw the woman turn, her eyes catching the scant light from those high windows. Not startled. Maybe not the first time she had been interrupted in her visits here.

"Yes?"

"I'm Lady Mortimer. I'm sorry to dist—"

"I know who you are," said Christabel, easing off the pew, and walking towards her.

As if this was not the place for questions to be asked and answered, Christabel took Kat's arm and gently led her out into the light.

HARRY SAT BACK and took notes as Bill Protheroe revealed the rumours he'd heard about the *true* nature of the Wetherby estate.

Major Wetherby, so it was said, had been a canny and highly successful investor in the years before the Great War, trading in stocks and shares. Much of his profits from these complex investments had been ploughed back into the lands and buildings of the estate.

But when the residue of his investments was added up after his own and his sons' deaths, it came nowhere near the amount expected.

A significant amount of funds had simply gone... missing.

"Missing?" said Harry, when Bill finished his tale. "How so, missing?"

"Well, there was no trace of it at all when the estate came to be valued for death duties. At the time – around 1916, I believe – I heard that, those funds being somehow unaccounted for, the lawyers for the Wetherby daughters had agreed to make a substantial and undisclosed tax payment in exchange for the family avoiding prosecution."

"Really? Isn't that tantamount to admitting the Major had stashed some large amount of money away to avoid tax?"

"Exactly," said Bill.

Harry had an important thought: *At last, a motive.* Then an important question: "I don't suppose these rumours extended to speculation about where the old fellow hid said loot?"

"Unfortunately *not*," said Bill. "And if I knew that, I wouldn't be here slaving over a hot printing press every Thursday night!"

Harry thought about what Bill had just told him.

"You think anyone in the family, either of his two daughters, knows where the money is?" he said.

"Well, if they do they've not touched it," said Bill. "You've seen the state of the Grange. And Christabel Taylor hardly lives in a mansion, I can tell you."

"So, you think that the money's gone forever?"

Harry saw Bill shrug.

"Come on, Bill. There's something you're not telling me."

Harry waited while Bill took out his pipe, and began re-packing it with fresh tobacco, before lighting it, and puffing away.

"All right," he said. "But – again – you *didn't* get this from me."

"Of course."

"Word is, that just before the Major went back to France for the last time, in '15, he hid the money somewhere, and told the two sons exactly where."

"In case he didn't make it home?"

"Exactly. But he wasn't to know or expect that his boys would also die within a day of his own demise."

"But doesn't that mean the secret died with them?"

"You would think so, wouldn't you?"

"But you don't?"

"One last rumour. Though it could simply be the idle chatter of over-interested locals…" Harry waited. "That rumour? That somehow Alice *knows* where the money is."

"But *not* Christabel?"

"No love lost between them, is there?" said Bill.

And Harry now understood why: the two women trapped in poverty, while one of the sisters maybe had the key to escape.

But – here was the inexplicable thing – for some reason was *not* willing to use it.

"Out of interest," Harry said. "How much are we possibly talking about here?"

"Oh," said Bill. "I can only speculate. But I would guess, around… fifty thousand pounds?"

Harry's mouth dropped open.

That sum… a small fortune.
And if true?

No wonder Bellamy Smythe had sought out Alice Wetherby in Brighton, and pursued her ever since.

Then there was another very important question.

If that was Smythe's game, *who was helping him?*

CHRISTABEL HAD THE air of a woman who had accepted what her life had become. Not for her the belief in the "other side" that so animated her sister Alice.

Her faith clearly lay in a more *conventional* spirit world.

They had sat together on a low marble bench outside the mausoleum, and Kat explained her concerns about Alice, and why she and Harry had gotten involved. Christabel listened, nodded.

But while she was worried about her "gullible sister" she didn't really see any apparent reason to be terribly concerned.

"After all," Christabel said, "what does she have to lose?"

Kat nodded at that, somehow sensing that between these two sisters there must be secrets.

But also feeling that Christabel was being deliberately evasive.

"But Christabel, is there nothing of value that your sister *might* have that someone like Smythe *could* want?"

At that, the sun on the woman's face, lined way too early with loss and worry, she smiled.

"You have seen *how* we live, Lady Mortimer. There is barely enough for the upkeep of our homes."

"I can imagine it must be difficult," said Kat. There was another question she wanted to ask – and no easy way to ask it. "I wonder – sorry – but is there a reason why Alice lives in the Grange, and you in your cottage?"

The angry reaction was instant, and Kat saw Christabel whip round to face her.

"The circumstances of my inheritance are *not* part of this discussion, Lady Mortimer."

Touché, thought Kat. *So there is something going on here.*

"My apologies," she said. "I'm just trying to work out Bellamy Smythe's possible motive for dragging your sister into these séances."

"I have absolutely no idea. I assure you, it cannot be money. What little money we *did* have, my sister has squandered on her futile quest to make contact with my father."

"You don't believe in spiritualism?"

"No. Not at all."

"But you did agree to go to the séance with Alice?"

"Of course. To protect her — she is still my sister. And my daughter, who insisted on being there too."

"You disapprove of your daughter's decision?"

"Diana is old enough to make her own mind up."

Kat took a breath.

"Christabel — Alice truly believes that your father spoke to you both that night."

"She does. *I* do not. It was utter nonsense."

"But Smythe knew some words... pet words from your childhood, no?"

Kat watched carefully, and she saw Christabel shift uncomfortably.

"Yes. But about all that? I just don't *know.*"

"Alice seemed convinced by it. And how could Bellamy possibly know?"

"How do charlatans do such things? Maybe the man just made a lucky guess, that is all?"

"A guess lucky enough to convince your sister," said Kat. "Enough for her to set up another séance tonight. Will you be attending?"

"Certainly not," said Christabel. And now she looked away.

From here, one could see down towards the town, to the roof of the Grange, just beyond where the woods ended and gave way to meadow.

Her sister's house, always in sight.

Kat gazed at her. Christabel was hiding something – but what? Was it possible – could she be involved in some scam here, against her own sister? *Envious of Alice's larger house? Wanting to level the playing field somehow?*

Then Christabel turned back to Kat.

"I believe this conversation has run its course, Lady Mortimer," she said. "If you would be so kind as to leave me now to my devotions."

Kat stood and watched as Christabel got up and walked back into the darkness of the mausoleum.

Clearly, she had a secret.

But what was it? And what did it have to do with Bellamy Smythe and his interest in Alice Wetherby?

Kat didn't have an idea. Not yet.

She started back down the trail to the car, thinking through what she just heard, and wondering whether Harry had discovered anything at all on his own journey to the past, through the back issues of the *Mydworth Mercury*.

HARRY EMERGED FROM the dusty offices of the *Mercury* onto Old Lane, and waited while Bill Protheroe locked up behind him.

He took in the afternoon air: the sounds of the festival floating down from the square; the smell of cooking emanating from all the stalls, reminding him it was already late for lunch; the scattered groups of townsfolk, many in costume, lounging on street corners, bustling to or from the pubs.

"Fancy a quick pint, Harry?" said Bill.

"Would absolutely love to, Bill," said Harry. "But this business I'm dealing with is pressing. More questions than answers. Need a clear head today, I fear."

"Well good luck, old man. Whatever is going on, this Smythe chap sounds a dodgy piece of work."

They shook hands and Harry turned to walk back up the street towards home.

"Hold on, Harry," called Bill, and Harry waited while Bill walked closer. "Just remembered – we had someone else in the archive a month or so back, going through those very same folders, those years."

"Go on," said Harry, intrigued.

"Funny chap – funny as in, always cracking jokes. Now, what was his name…?"

And Harry thought: *Maybe my luck with all this is finally changing:*

"Let me guess," said Harry. "Abel Coates?"

"Right! That's the one! Odd name I thought. Didn't seem like the researching type either!"

"Bill, what you just remembered might be very helpful."

"Oh, good. Think there's any connection with what *you're* up to?" said Bill.

"Who knows? Could be. I'll let you know."

They shook hands again, and Harry watched the newspaperman head off home.

Then he smiled to himself, and started home as well, his walk brisk.

Abel Coates had been researching Mydworth history. Unlikely that he was improving himself.

No. Much more probable that he was getting information for Bellamy Smythe.

And now a bit of hope: *was this the break he and Kat had been waiting for?*

A DISTANT VOICE

13.

SECRETS OF THE ACCOMPLICE

HARRY TURNED TO Kat, her face catching the afternoon light through the open window of the Alvis, a gentle breeze blowing wisps of her hair.

It seems, he thought, *no matter where Kat is, the light finds her.*

"Nearly four o'clock," she said. "What time does Abel's shift at the pub start?"

"Four, apparently," said Harry, seated, like Kat, low in the car. "If my informant at the Station Inn is to be trusted."

"He's going to be late."

Harry looked across Quay Road at the tiny end of terrace cottage where Abel Coates lived.

They'd driven slowly down the road, the river just to their left, until they'd found a secluded little spot to pull in. The kind of place, just on the edge of the town, that lovers might find to while away a sunny Saturday afternoon, uninterrupted.

But also, the perfect place from which to observe someone who was now a suspect — with a little breaking and entering planned for later.

"Aha," said Harry, seeing the door to the cottage open. "Curtain up!"

He watched as Abel Coates stood in the doorway, putting on his jacket. But then the man turned — and spoke to somebody in the house, somebody they couldn't see.

"Dammit," said Harry. "He's got visitors. Thought he lived on his own."

They waited and watched, the seconds ticking by.

Then a second figure emerged – a woman, carrying a shopping bag.

"Well, *waddya* know," said Kat. "Maeve O'Connor."

"She a lodger, maybe?" said Harry. "Good friend? Or something more interesting?"

"Ha! Doubt she's there to cut his hair."

Then he saw Abel embrace the woman, hold her tightly, the pair of them laughing together.

"Well, there you go, Harry. More than a lodger, that's for sure," said Kat. "Uh-oh, careful – they're heading this way."

Harry leaned over to Kat, pulled her tight and they kissed. In the carefully positioned vanity mirror he watched Abel and Maeve pass by on the other side of the road.

When they'd gone, he sat up.

"You know, we should do this more often," he said. "Has a rather exciting, illicit feel to it, right?"

"I'll put it in my diary for next Saturday," said Kat, smiling. "Meanwhile…" She pulled out a penny from her purse. "Heads or tails?" she said, spinning the coin.

"Heads."

"Tails, it is."

"You always get all the fun," said Harry. "Want to borrow my picks?"

"Brought my own," said Kat, taking a small leather pouch from her handbag.

"I'd suggest… don't be very long. I suspect Maeve's just popping out to the shops before they close."

He watched, as Kat climbed out of the car.

"Toot the horn if you see her," she said.

"Will do," said Harry.

He watched her cross the road and head towards Abel Coates's house.

Back in their mutual "diplomatic" postings, on various duties across Europe and beyond, both he and Kat had had need of some irregular and – if caught – disavowable skills in their undercover work for their separate governments.

A DISTANT VOICE

So – he knew it would be but a work of seconds for her to slip open the average Mydworth front door.

KAT PUSHED OPEN the cottage door, and quickly closed it behind her. As she'd expected, the lock hadn't proved a challenge at all.

She took in the tiny dwelling. The door opened straight into a living room, with a tight staircase that led up, and a small kitchen and scullery behind. Beyond that, she spotted a door leading out to a garden.

She went through to the scullery, unlocked the door, stepped out past the outside toilet. The garden – no more than the smallest back yard – had a wall on one side, but a low fence of chicken wire on the other: if needed, she now had an escape route.

Abel Coates didn't seem – so far – a threat. But then again – if there were large sums of money in play, as Harry had suggested there might be, who knew what he was capable of?

She left the back door ajar, stepped back into the kitchen and looked around. A teapot, two mugs. On the drying rack two plates.

In the living room – signs that this house was more likely occupied by two than one.

Were Maeve and Abel a couple?

Quickly, efficiently, she worked her way around the living room, opening drawers, checking, looking for papers.

Apart from a few bills, there was nothing.

She went to the window, looked out. So quiet. No sign of movement on the street.

She turned back into the room, went to the front door and locked it again with her pick.

Just in case...

Then she took the narrow wooden stairs.

AT THE TOP, two doors – two bedrooms.

She opened the one to the rear. To see: boxes piled on a small truckle bed, a desk, a small cupboard.

Then she opened the other door – to the main bedroom at the front of the cottage. She stepped in, searched the only furniture – a rickety looking wardrobe, a chest of drawers.

Inside, clothes for a man – and a woman. So though Nicola had given her a different address for Maeve, it was clear the hairdresser lived here... for at least some of the time.

But beyond the woman's clothes, some make-up items and hair brushes, Kat could see nothing unusual. She stepped to the window, edged open a corner of the net curtain, looked down the road: she could see Harry in the Alvis.

No sign of Maeve returning. But that didn't mean anything.

In and out in ten, that had always been her rule when it came to break-ins.

Five minutes left to find something. Time to check the rear bedroom.

HARRY CHECKED HIS watch, then a movement in the car mirror caught his eye. He turned to look over his shoulder to see a figure hurrying down the road towards him.

Maeve O'Connor, returning already!

He reached forward to hit the horn.

But then, a door in one of the other cottages opened – and a woman stepped out, called to Maeve.

Harry paused – his hand on the button, ready to press.

The hairdresser stopped – and the two chatted for a few seconds – Maeve looking up and down the street as if uncertain what to do.

Then Harry saw her smile at the woman and the two of them disappeared into the cottage.

A helpful spot of tea offered, perhaps?

Harry breathed again and settled back into his seat, eyes pinned on the cottage.

KAT OPENED UP the first of the boxes in the small bedroom and knew straight away she had found something important.

The label clear: *Artificial smoke canisters.*

She read the details: *"Theatrical use only. Noiseless. Odourless. Leaves no oily residue."*

Not the kind of thing your average barman or hairdresser carries in their luggage, she thought. *But perfect if you're setting up a phony séance.*

In the next box: costumes, uniforms, hats, wigs, moustaches. Packets of fishing line. A tin can filled with small brass hooks – *just like the one that Harry had found under the table at the Grange.*

And in the next: more theatrical pyrotechnics. Lurid cartons proclaimed the unique properties of the contents: *"Loud as wartime mortars! Flashes like an artillery barrage! Guaranteed heart-stoppers!"*

But then, in another crate, something unexpected.

Truncheons, brass knuckles, batons. Then – more sinister – what looked like a working Webley revolver. Beside it, a flare gun. And to complete this intimidating set, a trio of some very nasty looking sheath knives.

This was an armoury. For show? *Or would Abel resort to such weapons if things started to go wrong?*

Kat realised that seeing this, the level of danger – and fear warranted – had now shot *way up*.

She put the lids back on the boxes, knowing she was running out of time.

Then, she went over to the desk, pulled open every drawer – but saw only a few bills, receipts, ticket stubs. Her every instinct told her that somewhere here there must be evidence linking Abel to Bellamy – and to the victims.

Clock ticking.

In the corner of the room – a tall wardrobe, a chair in front of it. She moved the chair away – opened the doors. Empty.

Then she realised: *the chair belonged in front of the desk.* There was no reason for it to be here in the corner of the room, taking up space.

She put the chair back, stood on it and reached up onto the top of the wardrobe, felt around until…

Yes.

Her hand touched on a book of some kind. She lifted it down – some kind of hefty ledger, the kind of thing an accountant might use.

Quickly, she took it to the window for light: at the front was an index – a list of towns, separated by county. She flicked through the pages.

Inside, carefully annotated in different inks and hands, she saw page after page of handwritten columns, listing names, background, occupation, family.

Kat knew instantly what this was.

Right here, a list of past and potential victims, the result perhaps of months, maybe even years of chatting, talking, listening, scouring for information, for juicy tips to fortunes, cash, inheritances.

Chillingly, she saw that against each family, in the final column – a sum had been written, again in a careful copperplate hand.

Fifty pounds. A hundred pounds. Five hundred pounds.

The projected "winnings", she guessed. The financial reward for conning all these bereaved, mourning individuals and families across the south of England.

Abel Coates, you are one coldhearted bastard, thought Kat. *And – rest assured – Harry and I are going to destroy you.*

Kat was about to turn the pages to Mydworth, when she heard a sound outside that she recognised.

The briefest of toots from the Alvis horn.

And, almost immediately, the *clank* of the garden gate outside.

No time to think. She grabbed the ledger, tucked it under her arm, and *raced* down the stairs.

She could hear a key already in the lock of the front door.

Locking that door again had given her vital seconds.

She tore through the scullery, and out of the kitchen door, pulling it shut just as the front door slammed.

A DISTANT VOICE

Then, crouching so as not to be seen from the kitchen, she half crawled, half ran, to the wire fence at the side of the garden and clambered over, rolled away, just – a quick look over her shoulder – as Maeve O'Connor appeared at the back of the cottage, peering out. Presumably to see what had caused the noise.

Kat froze, peering through the wire of somebody's chicken hutch, waiting, breathing hard; the smell of the birds and their droppings making her eyes water.

At last, she saw the woman mutter something to herself and go back inside.

Kat gave it another minute, then got up, brushed her clothes down, a few feathers flying away, and walked down the path to Quay Road, as if in no rush at all.

Too risky to climb into the Alvis: instead she walked past Harry, gave him the slightest of winks, and carried on up the road into the village.

Behind her, she heard him starting up the car.

She smiled to herself, imagining what he must have been going through over the last few minutes.

The watching and waiting – and worrying – always more stressful than the doing!

14.

IS THERE ANYBODY THERE?

HARRY SLOWLY TURNED over the pages of the ledger, in the late afternoon sun, pausing every now and then to jot things down in his notebook resting on the little wrought iron table.

"Harry. With this, and all those weapons, you think it's time to go to the police?" said Kat.

He looked across the table at his wife: the roses blooming on the trellis framed her perfectly.

The garden of the Dower House at the very height of its Midsummer glory.

"Does seem sensible, doesn't it? We've certainly got enough here to prove this little gang have been duping people for months," he said. "Veritable *Who's Who* of Mydworth by the way. Did you see we're even in here too?"

"I did," said Kat. "I like the note in red ink next to our names – 'avoid if possible'."

Harry laughed. "And here was I thinking we were a perfectly admirable couple. It seems our reputation as troublemakers precedes us."

"Right," she said, laughing. "You see Alice Wetherby was underlined?" said Kat, leaning across the garden table and turning a page. "And the figure in that final column, exactly matching what Bill told you at the *Mercury*."

"Fifty thousand, yes. Nice work, if you can get it, eh?"

"So, back to the question then: the police, or not the police?"

"Well, there's definitely enough here to charge Abel, and probably Bellamy too, even Maeve. But, we *do* that and I doubt we'll get the answer to the bigger question we've been asking."

"Who's been helping them on the inside? Who's the source?"

"Exactly. Who told them about the lost money? And also, there's no guarantee right now that this little scam against Alice would even go to court. I mean, so far, I doubt there's even been a chargeable offence."

"All right – so we carry on with the plan then?" said Kat. "Infiltrate tonight's séance? In whatever way you say we can do that?"

"I think so. If the rumour is correct, that Alice knows where the loot is—"

"And Bellamy's mob clearly think she does."

"Yes. Well, I imagine tonight's the night they'll try and get her to reveal the whereabouts."

"Any idea how Bellamy will do that?"

"None whatsoever," said Harry, laughing again. "I imagine it will be entertaining to see how he tries!"

"And, as to your idea how we actually get into the séance...?"

"Oh, now *that*. See, that I do know how to do. But we have a few hours to kill. So, first – cocktails I think, then a spot of dinner. Can't go séance-busting on an empty stomach, eh?"

Kat grinned. "You do like to keeping me waiting, don't you?"

"Why sometimes... *ab-so-lutely*!"

THE TOWN HALL clock was chiming eight by the time Kat and Harry crossed Market Square on their way to the Grange.

Kat had never seen the square so packed with people – nor had she ever encountered such a bizarre atmosphere.

It was as if she'd been transported to a strange medieval fayre, with a jumble of jesters, mummers, bands, barrels of ale, dancing, food stalls, and even fire-eaters.

And now, as well as the hooded prancing around with their horse heads, others were wearing outlandish animal masks, and there were real horses too, ridden by "knights" in full armour, fearsome and tall as they steered their mounts through the crowds.

For someone born and raised in the Bronx, all of it was something to see.

"You know, next year we must dress up too and join in," said Harry as they slipped into an alleyway to avoid the crush. "All jolly good fun. I mean, when you are not busy trying to catch bad guys."

"I'll take your word for that," said Kat, relieved to be out of the throng.

As they turned, she saw that Spa Road was quiet. And as they walked down the leafy lane in the growing dusk, she could barely believe they were just minutes from the wacky mayhem in the centre of town.

"At least it's quiet down here," she said.

"For now," said Harry. "Another couple of hours and you won't be able to move along this lane. See Myers Hill up there?"

Kat looked up to her right, to the distant wooded slopes where she knew the mausoleum stood.

"Top of that hill is a jolly great bonfire, all waiting to be lit. And this is the road they take to get up there."

They carried on walking, but just before they reached the Grange, Harry stopped and she saw him turn to look at the bushes at the side of the road.

"Um, wait. I think… just around here… Yes!"

He stepped into the hedge, held back the branches and beckoned to her. She stepped past him – and saw a small gate leading into a field.

Together they went through the gate, and then paused in the shadows. Because, just a hundred yards away, Kat could see a garden wall, and beyond it the shape of the Grange.

"See… this is the way the gang and I used to get in and out of the house, all in secret," said Harry, and Kat could see his face shining with excitement. "Over that wall, down the coal chute, into the cellars – won't take but a minute."

"Coal chute?" said Kat.

"I know! That's the absolute best bit! Come on!"

And off he went towards the far wall, crouched low. Kat smiled, shook her head, and followed.

A DISTANT VOICE

TEN MINUTES LATER, they were standing in darkness at the foot of the servants' staircase, the chute and the cellars behind them.

Harry turned to Kat and put his finger to his mouth. In a shaft of moonlight from a high window, she could see his cheeks smeared with coal dust and she knew her face must look just the same.

Not that she minded. In fact, it made them less likely to be spotted.

"Far as I know, there's just that Lance character we need to worry about back here," he said. "Maggie said they don't even have a cook."

"Harry – hang on. You hear *that?*" whispered Kat. She could just make out Bellamy's voice somewhere in the house. "I think they're here already."

Harry stopped, listened.

"I do believe you're right. But don't worry, we're nearly there."

"Where are we now?" said Kat.

"Let's see. Drawing room and dining room *that* way," said Harry, pointing down the servants' hallway. "But we're going this way – to the old upstairs scullery. If it's still where I *think* it is."

And Kat followed him, as he led the way down the corridor in the evening light, until he reached a plain, unmarked door.

"Fingers crossed and all that," he said, as Kat joined him.

She watched as he reached down, turned the handle gently and pushed the door open.

KAT SAW HARRY beckon her inside, then shut the door. She looked around, her eyes adjusting to the almost total darkness in here: the room was empty, apart from a small kitchen sink, a table, shelves with plates and glasses.

"I imagine they used to use this room for serving to parties, dinners and so on. But we loved it for a different reason. Spying on the grown-ups! Great fun. I'll show you."

He walked over to the wall and Kat saw him reach across to a small serving hatch. Carefully, silently, he slid it open just *half an inch*, then gestured to her to peer through.

She came close, put her eye to the opening: and saw the dining room where the séance would take place. The room was dark apart from a single candle burning in the centre of the table.

She stepped back and Harry shut the tiny door tight.

"Now – all we have to do is *wait*," he said.

AFTER A LONG twenty minutes, Harry finally heard voices from the dining room, and saw a sliver of light through the serving hatch doors.

He recognised Bellamy's voice – and Alice's; but nobody else. He heard the sound of chairs being moved, then the light faded to a flicker: clearly only the single candle now illuminated the drawing room.

He reached forward and slid the serving hatch door back, far enough that he and Kat could just about see through without being seen.

He'd expected there to be a full house again, around the table. But now he saw, in the darkness, only Bellamy and Alice, a lit candle between them.

No Abel, Maeve, Diana or Christabel.

Interesting.

The curtains were closed, but Harry could just make out wisps of fog drifting through from the French windows, making a swirling layer above the carpet.

Fog on a summer's night? He had to smile at that – but there was no doubt that Bellamy's theatrics added to the sense of the spirit world so close.

"Midsummer's Eve!" said Bellamy suddenly, breaking the silence. "The one night of the year when you can be sure that the spirits will break through and make their wishes known!"

Harry saw Alice take a deep breath, placing her hand to her breast.

"Are you ready, Alice?" continued Bellamy, softly now. "Are you ready to reach out to the other side?"

"I am!"

At this, the candle fluttered and sparked.

"And – please say – who do you wish to speak to tonight, Alice?"

Harry saw Kat roll her eyes at the theatrics and he smiled at her in the half light.

We all know by now who Alice wants to talk to, he thought.

"My father," said Alice. "My beloved father."

Bellamy nodded. Then, Harry saw the medium raise his eyes to the ceiling: "Are you *here* with us tonight, Major Wetherby? If you are, give us… a sign."

The tiniest of movements by the curtain caught Harry's eye. Whoever was out there, was now tugging on a thread or fishing line that must lead to the table.

And yes, there was the response: *Tap, tap, tap!*

"Is that the Major speaking to us? One tap for 'yes', two for 'no'."

Tap.

Harry heard a sharp intake of breath and a low moan from Alice.

"Major! Do you wish to speak to your daughter, Alice? She is right here."

Tap.

"You do? Then make yourself known! The moment is nigh!"

And, at that, the candle flared brightly, the windows and doors rattled on cue – and from outside the room Harry heard a screeching howl that wouldn't have been out of place in the Mydworth Players' recent performance of Macbeth.

Is that Maeve supplying tonight's chorus? he thought.

With Kat's face pressed close to his – *not unpleasant this*, he thought – he peered through the hatch into the room, as Bellamy now tilted his head back, rolled his eyes into his skull and spoke, his voice *shifting*:

"Alice? *Alice?* Is that you my bonny child?" came Bellamy's voice, but now strange, filtered, strangulated.

Clever, thought Harry. *He's palmed some kind of voice modulator into his mouth.*

"Daddy! Daddy, yes, I'm here! Yes!" called Alice, and Harry saw her peering at the ceiling as if the Major himself was about to appear.

"You are so beautiful, my daughter," said the voice. "You have become a fine woman."

"I miss you, Daddy, I miss you so much."

"Fear not, darling. I am always here – always with *you.*"

"Oh, Daddy."

"But my child… look at you. At this house. You have fallen on hard times."

"I survive, Daddy, we survive. I get by. It is not important."

"But it is, child, it is."

Harry looked at Kat. She nodded.

Bellamy not hanging around here, but getting straight to the point.

"No! You should be living well. I left plenty for you, for your comfort and prosperity. Your brothers, *they* were to take care of you!"

Alice didn't answer, and Harry wondered what Bellamy's strategy would be.

"We must talk of the secret I told you about, my dear Alice. We must talk of that… money."

Again, no answer from Alice.

"Fear not, my child," said the voice, now becoming insistent. "Nobody can hear us here. We are safe. And our shared spirit guide will have no memory of what passes between us now."

That's a clever twist, Harry thought. *But will it work?*

"You are sure, Daddy?" said Alice, a hint of concern noticeable in her voice.

"I am."

"As you told me, I have not touched the money, Daddy."

"That is good. You were always such a good girl, Alice."

"And as you instructed me, I never told Christabel."

"You are true to your word indeed. So the money – it is still... safe? In... *in the secret safe place?*"

"Yes."

"Excellent," said the voice, and Harry could almost hear the relief from Bellamy.

"I know that money was not for me or for Christabel," continued Alice. "It is to be safeguarded for future generations. As you instructed."

"That is true, child. That *is* what I instructed. But now, I see your poverty. *Your* need. When your brothers did not return, things changed for you!"

"I–I can bear it, Daddy."

"No! You must not. You *will* not. You must go – to the safe place. Take the money. Share it with your sister. Rebuild the house. Make the Grange grand once again!"

"But your instructions...?"

"Now listen, my bonny girl... you now know that these are my new instructions. You must do as I say. Go to the safe place. Get the money. Tonight."

Then Harry heard, as if to be perfectly clear.

"Now!"

"But, Daddy, I don't know if—"

"Tonight."

"It will not be easy, Daddy, not easy for me after so many years, staying quiet, as you asked—"

"Midsummer's Eve, my child. Oh... oh... I am fading already."

"What? Daddy! Daddy, don't go!"

"The veil is closing again, my beloved. Remember my wishes *now*. Do as I say – or my soul shall never float free—"

"Daddy!" cried Alice, and Harry saw her stand, as – with perfect timing – there came a loud flash and a crack of thunder from outside the windows, and the table rocked and clattered back and forth.

Bellamy flung his head forward, then cried out, clutching his hands to his head dramatically.

"Don't leave me, Daddy!" called Alice as the candle roared improbably into full flame a foot high, and Bellamy slumped from the table to the ground.

Harry saw the door into the dining room now burst open as if of its own accord. And he just caught a glimpse of a figure out there, diving out of view, though who it was, he couldn't tell.

Then, as if she had been commanded by the spirit world (*which in a sense she had*) Alice quickly backed away from the table, turned, and ran out of the room, her arms flailing.

Harry had barely time to look at Kat for her reaction, when the electric light in the dining room clicked on.

Quickly Kat slid the serving hatch door almost shut – with just enough of a crack for them both to peer through – as the room seemed – almost impossibly and comically quickly to fill with people, *like the final, hectic scene of one of those Whitehall farces he used to go to years back.*

From behind the curtains, Abel appeared, grinning!

Bellamy grabbed the table and pulled himself up, his head swivelling maniacally!

Maeve O'Connor popped out from behind a cupboard!

"Well? What the hell are you waiting for?" hissed Bellamy at the barman whose grin faltered. "Follow her, you idiot!"

Abel shot out of the room in pursuit of Alice, as Bellamy now turned to Maeve: "And you – clean this up mess, dammit. Not a trace to be left, you hear me?"

Meanwhile, Harry heard doors slamming from deep within the house and voices shouting.

At which, Bellamy also ran out of the room.

Harry turned to Kat, just visible in the darkness.

"Well, Kat, I do believe that's *our* cue," he said.

"I think you're right," said Kat. "But what – where – and who?"

"Looks like we'll have to improvise."

"Isn't that what troublemakers do?" said Kat.

"Your strong point, if I remember correctly."

And together they raced for the door – and an unknown pursuit.

To follow Alice as she in turn raced to retrieve the money.

The Wetherby fortune.

15.

LET THE SURPRISES BEGIN!

AT THE END of the servants' corridor, Harry pulled open the door into the main hallway – then stopped dead as Kat joined him.

"I don't hear anything, do you?" he said, peering up at the staircase in the gloom, the darkness broken only by a distant electric light in a corridor.

"Where did she go?" said Kat.

Then, from the back of the house, he just heard the sound of a door banging.

"The garden?" said Kat.

"Or beyond" said Harry. "There's a gate – leads up to the woods."

Kat turned to him – and he could see from her face that she had an idea…

"Harry – you follow Abel and Alice. Meanwhile I'll inform that lot back there that the game is *nearly* over."

"They may not take too well to *that* news."

"Don't worry. I've dealt with worse."

"I know you have."

Just as he was about to go, she reached close and kissed him. "Harry, be careful."

"You too, Lady Mortimer, you too."

And then he moved as fast as he could, to get out of the house and onto Abel's trail.

HARRY SPRINTED ACROSS the overgrown lawn at the rear of the Grange, and out through an old rusty gate into a field that rose gently to woods, and beyond to Myers Hill.

Darkness had fallen, but in the light of a rising moon, he could just see the figure of Alice, bearing a lantern, disappearing into the trees.

Behind her, he saw Abel, hugging the scrubby bushes dotting the meadow... so if she'd look back, Alice would see nothing.

What Abel *didn't* know was that Harry was now doing exactly the same with him.

As the gap narrowed between them, he spotted that Abel had covered his face; no matter what was about to happen, he was taking care not to be recognised.

But also, Abel held something in his right hand. It was impossible to see exactly what it was – on the dark trail, the low moon scarcely lighting it – but Harry knew it couldn't be *good*.

Harry had a gun back in the Alvis. Since his return to Mydworth, it seemed like a reasonable precaution for all that he and Kat were up to.

But there was no time to go back for that.

Be careful, he had said to Kat.

Time to take my own prescription, he thought as he followed Abel into the dark woods.

KAT PUT THE phone back in its cradle, having informed Sergeant Timms that the enthusiastic Midsummer revellers weren't his *only* problem tonight.

Then she entered the dining room and took in the messy aftermath of the séance.

Easily seen now, all the gimmicks used to create the effects, like the French doors that flew open after a good yank, the unseen fishing line that made a metal item tap on the table at just the right moment.

Maeve O'Connor stood by the table, wiping down the candlestick, probably to make sure that there were no signs of the flashing explosive that had been triggered so dramatically. Smythe was partly under the table.

For a moment – amazingly – they didn't notice Kat, so busy were they with their cleaning and clearing.

So, she started. "Don't think you have to worry about *any* of that," she said.

Smythe popped out, troll-like, from under the table.

"Wh-what are you doing here? I told you, that this – tonight was—"

"Save it, Smythe. Sir Harry and I saw it *all.*"

That got Smythe popping up and looking around the disarrayed room as if Kat's husband had perhaps turned himself invisible.

"Sir Harry?"

"Oh – no worries. He's after your other accomplice. Just yards behind him, I imagine. Abel Coates planning on surprising poor Alice, while – *imagine that* – my Harry's about to surprise him."

Bellamy Smythe's face turned dark at this. "He doesn't know who he's fooling with."

For a second those words chilled Kat. But she simply nodded. "My husband can handle himself. As for you two—"

She saw that O'Connor had taken a step with the candlestick, and she was holding it in a very different way.

Almost as if it had turned from candlestick to weapon.

"Oh, Maeve, how about you stop right there? Hate to see you get hurt. And I'm sure the two of you are very curious to know what is going to happen next."

Both her victims' mouths were slightly agape – curious indeed.

"I've already called the police, by the way. They're going to be here *lickety-split*, as we say back home. Then this show of yours will truly be over."

Kat paused a second, gauging whether either of them was about to try something unfortunate, like dashing away or – even worse – an ill-thought attempt to start a fight.

That wouldn't end well, she knew.

A DISTANT VOICE

But though they were calculating the dwindling possibilities here, Kat guessed that they were probably strangers to physical violence.

Abel Coates though? That might be another story, judging from the arsenal she'd found in his cottage.

"Now then, if you wouldn't mind being patient for just a *few* more moments, while we wait for the law to arrive?"

She pulled out one of the dining chairs, and sat watching as they stood motionless. "Oh, *do* continue your cleaning. Place *is* rather a mess after all that nonsense of yours."

HARRY CREPT THROUGH the trees, seeing a clearing ahead – a patch of grass lit dimly by the moon. There was no sign of Abel – or Alice.

Dropping now almost to a crawl, he edged forward from tree to tree until he could see the clearing – but without danger of being seen himself.

Pressed hard against an old oak tree, he slowly peered round, to see a mausoleum – grand, almost like a temple.

He recognised it from the photo in the *Mydworth Mercury*: this was the Wetherby Mausoleum where Kat had found Christabel praying, just that morning.

He couldn't see Alice, but the ornate metal gate stood open.

Standing to one side of the gate, almost hidden in the shadows – Abel Coates.

Harry could see now what the man held in his hand. A small curved truncheon, the type used as often by the riff-raff on the more dangerous streets of London as by their opposites in the Metropolitan Police.

No gun. At least, no gun *visible.*

Harry was all set to step forward from his hiding place into the clearing.

But then – hurrying as if she'd just been ordered by her late father – he saw Alice step out through the gate from the mausoleum.

In her hand she held a box, just the type one might find in a bank vault. It must have been hidden somewhere in the mausoleum, Harry guessed.

Harry was about to make a run at Abel – but then Alice stopped and turned to pull the metal door shut behind her with her free hand.

Abel stepped out of the shadows to her side, raised the truncheon expertly above his head... and brought it down *fast*.

And that's all it took for Alice to crumple to her knees, the box flying out of her hands, tumbling onto the grass.

Harry could see that whatever talents Abel might have as a barman, they paled in comparison to his use of the small baton in his hand.

Harry imagined that Alice would recover. But she'd awaken to that box... gone.

At least that was certainly Abel's plan.

A plan that Harry couldn't let him get away with. He stepped out of his cover, and started walking to Abel – steadily, not rushing – all the time keeping his eyes locked on the man.

The next few minutes? Well, they would be interesting to say the least.

KAT STOOD AT the back door of the Grange and looked up towards the woods and the distant hill, somehow ominous in the light from the low moon.

Somewhere up there – Harry was possibly going head-to-head with Abel Coates.

Coates – maybe armed with a gun.

Smythe and O'Connor were no longer a threat: Sergeant Timms had turned up surprisingly quickly with one of his constables, and it had taken just seconds to persuade him that the pair were up to no good.

But while the police dealt with the arrest – Kat knew there was nothing she could do here. And everything she could do to help Harry.

A DISTANT VOICE

But how to reach him in time?

Then a flickering light caught her eye. She turned – to see a line of revellers coming up Spa Road, flares held high, drums banging, violins playing, hooeners…

The Midsummer revellers, heading for Myers Hill and the ceremonial pyre.

And suddenly – she had an idea.

AT FIRST, ABEL had actually started walking right in the direction of Harry and the path back.

But then he noticed that he was not alone – and he stopped dead in his tracks.

Wish I had popped my gun in my pocket, Harry thought, again.

"Hey there, Coates. What seems to be the problem here?"

"How did you—?"

"Oh, right. You don't *know*, now do you? Saw the whole thing. Been following you. Quite the tough guy – attacking a woman."

Abel took a step, a smaller one, towards Harry, towards the trail back.

"Get out of my way or I'll do the same to you."

At that Abel, raised the truncheon over his head.

"Now, Coates, I should warn you – this is not my *first* encounter with such an item."

Abel charged.

The lunge was easily side-stepped, as Harry feinted right, then moved left, leaving his right leg to catch Coates, and send him tumbling face down. Once again, the metal box – with its still-hidden treasure – ended up on the dewy grass.

Harry picked it up as Coates, winded, struggled to his feet.

"There. *That* feels better. And I would advise you not to try anything like that with me again. You see, I do know so *many* ways to hurt a chap like you. I think what I'd suggest now is we wait for Alice to *revive*, then we all walk back together to the house, where I am sure the police have already arrived—"

But then Harry heard something. A different sound, at first hard to place. Not the noises echoing from the top of the hill in the distance, with the great Midsummer bonfire now alight.

No – he could hear *steps*. But not the steps of people on the trail.

No – now he recognised the steady, even cautious thud, thud of *horses*.

KEEPING ONE EYE on Abel, and with his hand tightly on the metal box, Harry turned as two people rode into the clearing.

It was dark enough that he didn't recognise them at first. Not until they both stopped, slipped off their horses and started walking towards them.

Even before they spoke, Harry finally saw who they were, and realised that the evening's surprises were far from over.

"WELL, WELL. LANCE and Diana. Out for an evening's ride?"

And that, Harry knew, might have been a reasonable guess, were it not for the fact that Lance held something in his hand. And this time, it was no truncheon.

With the distance closing as Lance and Diana walked side-by-side towards him and Coates, Harry saw that Lance held in his hand a Webley revolver.

Pointed right at me, Harry thought. *Which makes sense, because, well, I'm the one currently holding the box.*

Harry looked at the unlikely couple, suddenly understanding how the final jigsaw pieces of the Bellamy scam fitted together.

Lance who had the run of the Grange, could uncover the secrets of the money. Diana, living in relative poverty, blocked from an inheritance by her stubborn aunt, probably setting the whole larcenous plan in motion.

After what seemed a very long wait, Lance spoke.

"Don't *either* of you move. I am a crack shot. Even at night, even at this distance."

A DISTANT VOICE

"I'll take your word for it, old chap," Harry said. "Thanks for the useful information."

Harry realised he didn't need to be concerned with Abel Coates anymore. And he pretty much suspected what would occur next.

But on that score, he was only *partly* correct.

16.

A MIDSUMMER CHASE

"PUT THE BOX on the grass, then give it a good kick in my direction," said Lance, his voice low, sinister.

Harry sensed that this lad who served as Alice's general factotum must have quite an interesting history in other areas, as yet undiscovered. Unfortunate encounters with local authorities perhaps?

We should have looked into that! he thought.

He started to bend over to place the box on the dewy grass.

"Diana, sorry, but my wife and I were under the assumption that you actually *cared* for your dear aunt?"

"I'll tell you what I care about much more, *Sir* Harry. Getting out of Mydworth with Lance, with all the money that the stupid woman kept hidden while the rest of us lived in *poverty*."

"I see. And there was I thinking that perhaps—" Harry had the box on the grass "—a father's last words to a daughter ought to carry some weight."

"Kick it over, Mortimer."

Harry looked at the distance between him and the couple, the weight of the box, whether he had any useful options with a well-placed kick.

But he calculated that he *didn't*, and the only result would be a bullet delivered by the self-professed crack shot, Lance.

"*Now*," said Lance. "I don't have all bloody night."

Harry nodded, and gave it a kick – just enough so it slid on the wet grass to within a yard of Lance.

Then he noticed something interesting.

Diana had walked over to pick up the box. But before she could, Lance went into a quick crouch, gun still pointed at both Harry and Abel, and scooped it up.

Harry could see on Diana's face, an odd look. Perhaps *confused?*

But that confusion wasn't destined to linger for long.

"OKAY, DIANA, DEAREST – why don't you join the others? All of you get nice and close so I don't have to wave my gun around."

Harry could see that Diana was frozen by both the command and what it meant. Her plan – to flee with Lance and whatever was in the box – was disappearing fast.

Lance – probably all along – clearly had other plans.

Then to emphasise his point: "Do it now!"

And Diana – looking at Lance and the gun – backed away, speechless. Until, just as she was within an arm's reach of Abel Coates: "You *used* me," she said, her voice low, almost spitting the words.

To which Lance replied, "We all get used."

Harry was still trying to think: was there a possible *move* here to stop Lance getting away? A chap like him, knowing the old roads and trails, on a good horse could very easily disappear forever.

He saw Lance walk over to Diana's horse, and hiss at it as he gave it a healthy slap on its haunches.

"Now you *get!*"

The mare, in no mood for more of the same, galloped away.

Lance smoothly slid a foot into a stirrup on his own horse – no amateur rider here – and in one quick move, pulled himself back into the saddle. He slipped the metal container into a saddlebag.

"I probably should say... *don't even think of following me.* But then, on foot, stuck here—" He laughed. "You don't have a choice."

And with that, he sharply snapped the reins and his horse, a black mare with a white streak, whipped around, and then bolted away.

At that, Harry turned to the two conspirators, guilty but left – as one might say – holding the bag. "Well, hasn't *this* been an evening of surprises."

He could see Coates's eyes darting left and right, perhaps calculating the risk of trying to run away versus pleading whatever would be his case.

"Steady there, Coates," said Harry, picking up the truncheon from the wet grass, and smiling. "Looks like Alice is stirring a bit. We'll all just walk back to the Grange. I'm sure my wife will have arranged for the proper authorities to ask you *so* many questions."

But there was to be one last surprise.

Again, the sound of horse hooves, coming fast, a full gallop.

That horse entered the clearing, looking like a great steed from the era of knights and castles, draped with a royal blue skirt featuring the emblem of St George, and armed with an impressive headguard featuring an ominous horn.

And there was even a sword strapped to the horse's saddle.

The horse so amazing to see, that Harry almost didn't notice the rider.

His wife, Kat Riley, aka Lady Mortimer, jerking this grand beast to a full stop as if she and her mount had been riding together for years.

Harry had one quick question before bringing her up to speed.

"Now wherever did you get *that*?"

"A very pleasant man in armour kindly allowed me to borrow it. And—"

"Oh, right. Well, Lance, you see, has 'absconded', I think is the term, with the cash Alice recovered."

"Where is he?"

Harry pointed towards Myers Hill.

"I believe the expression you use is… *he went thatta away*."

And without another word, Kat snapped the reins and the horse – despite being festooned for a grand medieval pageant of some kind – responded with a quick trot, heading up the hill.

To where, in the distance, the revellers had gathered around the flaming bonfire.

Only one thing, Harry thought, *I probably should have mentioned he has a gun.*

WITH ONLY THE light from the crescent moon to guide her, Kat had to guess which way to weave to avoid hitting any deep ruts that could send her now-charging horse tumbling down.

The horse, on the other hand, seemed pretty confident, as if he had done these trails *many* times. Kat leaned down close: "Doing great, boy. Just keep it up."

And she didn't even have to use the reins much to maintain her breakneck speed – the warhorse racing on its own accord.

Until – just ahead, not far from the bonfire and the milling crowds of revellers, exactly atop Myers Hill – she saw Lance, also racing away, weaving around the odd tree that dotted the hillside.

But just as she thought she was gaining on him, she saw him turn back. Point at her.

And then she realised: he wasn't pointing at all, but rather *aiming.*

Then a shot, and she heard the round smash into a tree just feet away.

That was close*,* Kat thought.

Suddenly the ruts and grooves of the trail at night had become the least of her worries.

She urged her horse to go faster, and she heard its hearty snorts that accompanied the full-out gallop.

Another shot, and Kat swore she could *hear* the bullet whizzing by her head.

This Lance – Alice's once rather ineffective servant – clearly quite the rider, *and* quite the marksman.

But Kat had no choice. She just hoped she could close the distance in time.

Until, Lance turned once more and now, with the distance between them so close, Kat knew he could hardly miss.

But Lance did miss something else.

An errant tree limb stretched out over the trail. Only a few feet, but just enough, as Lance – not looking ahead – rode right into it, and it swept him off his speeding horse as one might swat away a pesky insect.

Kat pulled back on the reins again. Her horse responded quickly, and the second they had stopped, she jumped down.

Just ahead, she saw how close they were to the bonfire. The great crowd of onlookers – some in masks, some in horse heads, and dominated by a giant puppet of a dragon – all looked on, their attention pulled away from the roaring fire by this even more interesting spectacle.

The blow to Lance had knocked him flat to the ground, with his gun yards away.

But, only winded, he was already scrambling towards it.

Kat ran back to her horse and pulled what looked like an authentic medieval sword from its scabbard, bound to the saddle.

Heavy sword held firmly in two hands, she walked briskly to Lance and pressed the point down at the base of his spine.

"I'd hold it right *there*. This sword may be old but – as I'm sure you can feel – the point... nice and sharp."

And like a worm skewered at the business end of a hook, Lance writhed a bit, but the metal tip had dug in *just enough* to stop him trying to get the gun.

Kat looked up at the crowd, who suddenly applauded as if this was part of the Midsummer festivities, a show with perhaps more to come.

Unfortunately for them – there was only this. Kat bowed graciously, and they clapped again. Then she leaned down to Lance and picked up the gun, sticking it into a pocket.

A DISTANT VOICE

"Now, I'm afraid the evening is not quite over, Lance. Sergeant Timms is waiting at the Grange. And I'm sure he'll want to talk with *you* most of all."

For a second, Lance acted as if he didn't know what to do.

Kat applied a bit more pressure with the sword tip. Just enough to make the man on the ground wince.

"Now – get up, and get moving."

As Kat got ready to lead her hapless prisoner off the hill top, past the cheering crowd and back to… well, she imagined, justice.

17.

JUST A QUIET SUMMER EVENING

KAT WATCHED AS Lavinia looked around their small garden at the back of the Dower House.

"You have done a *wonderful* job back here."

Kat took a moment to observe the garden in the soft evening sun, the small rows of plants, flowers and herbs looking almost magical in the light.

"All credit to your gardener," Kat said.

"Yes," Harry added, "he certainly brought some order back here."

"And brought some prizes home, too, from the Flower Show so I gather, Harry?" said Lavinia.

"Indeed," said Harry. "Though not the roses, this time. Pipped at the post by Nicola's heady blooms – I believe that's what the judges called them."

"Good for her," said Kat. "Especially after such a difficult week."

"Indeed," said Harry, lifting the wine from the chiller. "Aunt Lavinia – a little more of the Sancerre?"

Kat watched as Harry's aunt took a deep breath and then – decision made – extended her glass.

"You know, there are still one or two things, about all that happened, that I don't quite understand."

Kat saw Harry smile at that. Dressed in a crisp white shirt and tan trousers, his outfit caught the almost Mediterranean light.

She never did tire of looking at him.

"Well, you can join Sergeant Timms in that department," Harry said. "I had to actually write all the details down for him, as best we knew them."

"That doesn't surprise me. So, I think you said they were *all* involved?"

"Well," Harry said, "not Christabel. But otherwise, yes."

"And it was Diana who first brought this Smythe character to the attention of Alice Wetherby?"

"Yes," Kat said. "Amazingly, it all starts there. Diana knew her mother had suspicions there was a missing fortune. Then, knowing her aunt's interest in the occult and in seeing Smythe, she hatched the plan."

"Smart girl. She'd go far if wasn't facing a season or two in prison."

"Then, of course, Smythe had to involve his co-conspirators," Kat added.

"That nasty Mr Coates and the hairdresser. Pity I won't get a chance of having her work on my hair. She *did* seem to have talent."

"But," Harry went on, taking a sip of the dry white wine as he did. "Nobody really had a clear take on this Lance."

"Diana's boyfriend."

"Yes. Turns out he's got quite a history of trouble with the law. He persuaded Diana to form a plan for *just* the two of them."

Kat saw Lavinia smile. "I see. But then at the end he pulled a double-cross on the bright girl herself?"

"Exactly," Harry said.

"And poor Alice in the middle of it!"

"Well, Lavinia," Kat said, "*not* so poor. What was in the box were securities. Some shrewd investments made by the Major at the turn of the century. Very valuable then, worth a *fortune* now. Even after the tax man has taken his cut."

"Good for her! And for Christabel too. If that silly thing Diana hadn't been so greedy, she'd be all set as well."

"All of them facing charges of fraud, attempted theft and in Abel's case, outright assault," Harry said. "Bad days in court ahead for the lot, I imagine."

Kat saw Lavinia take another sip of the wine. Though a mild summer evening, a bit of a chill had started to creep into the air along with the dew.

Soon she imagined Harry would drive his aunt back to Mydworth Manor.

And then it would be – after some very busy and strange days – just the two of them again.

That – she was looking forward to.

But Lavinia, it seemed, had one more thing to ask about.

She turned and looked at them as she put her wine glass down.

"So, Midsummer in Mydworth is finally over, thank heavens. Things nice and quiet again." She paused. "You two have any plans?"

Kat saw Harry look over to her. A smile.

Because they certainly did have some plans.

She gave Harry a smile back.

Harry turned to his aunt. "What kind of *plans,* Lavinia?"

"You know, just plans, for the two of you, now that things are—"

Harry is clearly enjoying this, Kat thought.

"Well, since you have asked, and all that." He took a breath. "We are actually planning a grand trip to Kat's hometown."

"Really?"

Kat had wanted Harry to come to New York with her. So much for him to see.

There's a big part of me in that city, she had told him. *You'll love it.*

And yet, she was aware what it meant to him to travel once again, across the Atlantic – New York harbour, the destination. But no, he seemed to love the idea – bookings with Cunard to be made, a full itinerary to be planned.

Though Kat imagined those weren't exactly the kind of plans Lavinia was enquiring about.

A DISTANT VOICE

Harry continued. "I say, Aunt Lavinia, why don't you join us? To see New York City with our personal guide! A native!"

"Is that what I am?" Kat said, laughing.

Lavinia was quick to respond.

"I'd absolutely love to. But well, we'll see. My social calendar, you know, always so full."

And with that not quite settled, they all finished the last of the Sancerre, the evening nearly over, with Mydworth – indeed – finally quiet.

Though Kat knew, somehow, that never did seem to last for long in this little Sussex town.

NEXT IN THE SERIES:

CITY HEAT

MYDWORTH MYSTERIES #10

Matthew Costello & Neil Richards

Kat brings Harry across the Atlantic to New York for a planned whirlwind time in her home town – complete with a lavish suite at the Plaza. But when Teddy Crowther – grandson of a wealthy City magnate - is snatched by the mob, the pair is asked to help.

As Prohibition New York swelters in a heatwave, the Mortimers soon find themselves playing a dangerous game of cat and mouse, not just with the kidnappers, but also the rest of the Crowther family, all of whom have everything to gain – and maybe lose – if Teddy is found...

ABOUT THE AUTHORS

Co-authors Neil Richards (based in the UK) and Matthew Costello (based in the US), have been writing together since the mid-90s, creating innovative television, games and best-selling books. Together, they have worked on major projects for the BBC, PBS, Disney Channel, Sony, ABC, Eidos, and Nintendo to name but a few.

Their transatlantic collaboration led to the globally best-selling mystery series, *Cherringham*, which has also been a top-seller as audiobooks read by Neil Dudgeon.

Mydworth Mysteries is their brand new series, set in 1929 Sussex, England, which takes readers back to a world where solving crimes was more difficult — but also sometimes a lot more fun.